ETERNAL MOURNING

A TALON PACK NOVEL

CARRIE ANN RYAN

Eternal Mourning
A Talon Pack Novel
By: Carrie Ann Ryan
© 2017 Carrie Ann Ryan
ISBN: 978-1-943123-79-7

For more information, please join Carrie Ann Ryan's MAILING LIST.
To interact with Carrie Ann Ryan, you can join her FAN CLUB.

AUTHOR HIGHLIGHTS

"Carrie Ann Ryan knows how to pull your heartstrings and make your pulse pound! Her wonderful Redwood Pack series will draw you in and keep you reading long into the night. I can't wait to see what comes next with the new generation, the Talons. Keep them coming, Carrie Ann!"

–Lara Adrian, New York Times bestselling author of CRAVE THE NIGHT

"Carrie Ann Ryan never fails to draw readers in with passion, raw sensuality, and characters that pop off the page. Any book by Carrie Ann is an absolute treat."

–New York Times Bestselling Author J. Kenner

"With snarky humor, sizzling love scenes, and brilliant, imaginative worldbuilding, The Dante's Circle series reads as if Carrie Ann Ryan peeked at my personal wish list!"

—NYT Bestselling Author, Larissa Ione

"Carrie Ann Ryan writes sexy shifters in a world full of passionate happily-ever-afters."

—*New York Times* Bestselling Author Vivian Arend

"Carrie Ann's books are sexy with characters you can't help but love from page one. They are heat and heart blended to perfection."

—*New York Times* Bestselling Author Jayne Rylon

Carrie Ann Ryan's books are wickedly funny and deliciously hot, with plenty of twists to keep you guessing. They'll keep you up all night!"

—USA Today Bestselling Author Cari Quinn

"Once again, Carrie Ann Ryan knocks the Dante's

Circle series out of the park. The queen of hot, sexy, enthralling paranormal romance, Carrie Ann is an author not to miss!"

—*New York Times* bestselling Author Marie Harte

DEDICATION

To Viv.

Thanks for showing me my wolves again...and for knowing how to use a generator in the middle of a forest, at night, with no power, while it was raining.

ACKNOWLEDGMENTS

I started writing this book three days before Daniel died and I honestly didn't know if I was going to finish writing it. I stared blankly at the few chapters I already had done and wondered if Walker and Aimee's story was the right one to tell. Of all my books I had to write while I was numb and trying to find my new normal, the one with Eternal Mourning as a title was the one that it had to be.

Fate is a tricky mistress sometimes and my characters above all know this.

Eternal Mourning is a book about fate, hope, healing, opening your soul to chance, and knowing that sometimes the end isn't quite what you thought it would be.

I know I couldn't have written this book without the support and love of so many. Thank you Vivian Arend for sitting with me in a log cabin and giggling about magical bunnies and curses while we plotted the last three Talon Pack books. I am not only a fan of your shifters, but you made me a fan of my own again.

Thank you, Kennedy Layne and Stacey Kennedy, for being in my corner every damn moment and showing me I can still be a writer and love it, even when I kind of hate it.

Thank you Chelle for trusting me and allowing me to trust myself with Walker and Aimee's journey. They were so different and yet perfect for what I needed.

As always, thank you to my team, Chelle, Tara, and Charity for keeping my releases straight and smiling at me when I say, yet again, I have a new idea. You put up with so much.

Thank you again, Daniel, for everything. I think I'm always going to put you in these forwards, just saying. I know you hate it when I put the spotlight on you, but well, I love you and I couldn't have ever written a word without you. I miss you so damn much.

And thank you readers, for being some of the best readers EVER. I couldn't do what I do without you and know that I cherish each and every one of you.

~Carrie Ann

ETERNAL MOURNING

In the seventh book of the Talon Pack series from NYT Bestselling Author Carrie Ann Ryan, a Healer is forced to come to grips with the idea that he can't save everyone... including the woman he loves.

Walker Brentwood vowed to the moon goddess that he'd protect his Pack and Heal with every last ounce of his power. He's watched his siblings and cousin battle the worst circumstances to find love and is now afraid that the one woman who could be his might not have much time left. The rules of mating have changed, and Walker will do what he has to in order to protect the bonds that have eluded him for so long.

Aimee Reagan knows there's something wrong with her. She's known since the first time she found out shifters were real and magic existed. When the Talon Pack's enemy sets his sights on her, her battle to survive becomes even harder.

Walker and Aimee must turn to each other when the powers around them change and the paths that had been laid before them are no longer clear. But when their passion threatens a curse far older than anyone dreamed, they'll only have one chance to save something worth more than a mating bond. Their future.

PREY

AGONY RIPPED THROUGH HER. She threw her head back, letting the sweet taste of it swallow her whole. She was the wind, the air, the breeze along the trees, yet she knew there was more to it. The others would be searching for her soon, for that was what she'd always known. The longer she drew in what came naturally to her, the harder they would fall from what little they had left.

She wasn't the monster the others feared, the danger lurking in the dark that called out for the weak, searched for the prey. So she pulled in more, knowing not to take too much or what she craved would fade too soon.

There was another enemy in the fold now, one that would know who she was and what she'd done. She would have to hold tightly to the ties that wrapped around her soul and body or risk losing it forever once the enemy and her master found her.

But first, the prey needed to scream.

And the enemies would circle the wounded like the animals they were, and she would drink until there was no more.

Until there was nothing.

Again.

CHAPTER 1

WALKER BRENTWOOD LET out a slow breath, figuring as long as he didn't growl or brood like any of his other family members he'd do okay. The rain began to pick up around them, the drops hitting the leaves of the tall trees with little splats and sputters. The sound was almost soothing, as if it could rock the pups to sleep. The scents of ozone and forest filled the air, soothing his wolf. His family would probably find that idea weird since he was generally the calmest of them all, but he was still a wolf.

Because their wolves had scented rain in the distance, the mating ceremony had been moved to the wooden archway of one of the large den buildings. Given how deep the deck was, and the fact that, thankfully, there wasn't any wind, no one would get wet, and the mated couple could be blessed by their Alpha in peace.

Mitchell and Dawn truly deserved that after everything they had gone through to mate. Though most mating ceremonies happened soon after the couple completed their bond, his cousin and Dawn had decided to wait a bit since the world had almost crashed down around them right when they finally cemented their union.

Walker frowned as he remembered everything that had happened around the time the two had marked each other. He didn't know the specifics of their relationship or why they had decided to wait, but he'd been there when they were forced to save each other in the end.

The Pack had almost lost Dawn when the fire witch took her, but the outcome of that had brought Mitchell's new mate into the Talon Pack as one of their own. She was a Central Pack wolf no more, and no longer alone. She had the Talons.

And from the shy smile on her face when she looked up at her growly mate, Walker had a feeling she was just beginning to understand that.

Gideon, Walker's brother and Alpha, stepped up onto the bottom step that led into the house, so he stood just slightly above everyone else. Despite the fact that Gideon wasn't one of Walker's triplet brothers, his Alpha still looked a lot like him. They all had thick, dark hair that curled at the ends if it got too long—though their sister Brynn's was only slightly wavy. And the whole lot of them had the Brentwood blue eyes. A color he figured came from their Irish ancestors, who had traveled over to the western side of the continent a century before the rest of the world had figured out how to make the trek without dying. Wolves were strong for a reason, and keeping themselves secluded and spread over the land was only one of them.

Even Mitchell and Max—brothers themselves yet cousins to Walker—looked like the rest of them. Their paternal line was dominant in their genes, and sometimes, Walker wondered what their maternal line contributed.

He knew the answer, of course, but that only made him frown harder. Each of them had a gentler side that had been beaten out of them over the years under his father's rule as Alpha. Only his cousin Max had been able to keep his sense of innocence throughout the years. Technically, Max was older than Walker and his fellow triplets, Kameron and Brandon, but to them, Max had almost seemed younger with his exuberance and thirst for life. But the wolf had lost any sense of who he was before when he lost his arm and so much more during the final battle of the Unveiling over a year ago.

"If you keep frowning like that, you're going to scare

Dawn and her little friends away," Kameron whispered low enough that not even the wolves close to them would hear. As shifters, they had sharper senses than humans and used that to their advantage to not only survive but also *thrive*. They could see longer distances, even in the barest of moonlight in the dark, and they could detect prey from miles away if the wind caught the scent just right. They could also hear sounds across the spectrum from a great distance. It took willpower and training to learn to live peacefully with so many sights, sounds, and scents bombarding them on any given day.

Walker forced his thoughts away from what had almost cost his family and Pack everything and schooled his features. He was truly happy for Mitchell and Dawn, and it was only the direction of his thoughts that had made him look like a brooding bastard. He'd do well to think of what angered him later when in private, rather than worry Dawn or any of the humans who accompanied her.

He gave Kameron a tight nod as Gideon began speaking about the newly mated couple and forced his gaze from them and the three small humans who stood at Dawn's side. This wasn't a human marriage ceremony, so there was no need for pomp and circumstance. The ceremony itself was what cemented the bond within the Pack, though even that wasn't truly necessary. Some couples didn't need the entire Pack around them when they vowed their love, devotion, and pledges to one another. This time, however, with Dawn's past—or rather, the past of her Pack—the Talons had wanted to make sure everyone knew she was accepted within the den.

Walker's attention snagged on one of the three standing by Dawn, and he did his best to keep his wolf in check. Curious by nature, his other half needed to know the *whys* of existence and truth, yet Walker had a feeling this urgency within him when it came to the pale blonde at Dawn's side wasn't just curiosity.

Dawn had kept her wolf's existence a secret within the human world, even after the Unveiling where the idea of shifters—at least wolves—was revealed to the public. She had three human friends who she had become truly close to over the years, but she had only recently been forced to reveal who she was to them.

The three women, Dhani, Cheyenne, and Aimee, had surprised them all when they turned out to be stronger-willed than many of the wolves he knew within the Pack. They'd done their best to prove to Dawn that they would stand by her no matter what, and Walker was pleased that Dawn wouldn't truly be alone in a new den. Not that these three were Packmates, but they were welcome guests within the wards when they chose to visit.

And the fact that his attention kept snagging on one of

them in particular? Well, that was just something he would have to unravel later when others weren't watching.

The world had been shown the magic of wolves and witches, yet they were still in the dark when it came to some magics, such as demons and now...cat shifters. Walker wasn't sure what else was out there, and as a man who thought he knew the depths of what existed outside of humans, the idea that he truly had no clue worried him.

Then again, this wasn't the place to worry about that. Not when the couple in front of him was vowing their love to one another. He still wasn't quite sure how Mitchell had fallen so hard and fast for the quiet wolf standing by his side, but then again, fate and the moon goddess had their own plans when it came to the goddess's children.

"I promise to honor who we are together and who we can be," Dawn said softly. Walker wasn't watching her, however, as he still had his eyes on the pale blonde. The dark circles under Aimee's eyes were more pronounced, and she seemed to be listing to the side every so often until one of the other women brushed against her gently, causing her to stand straight again.

He held back a frown as she blinked hard a few times as if trying to keep herself focused and awake. There was something wrong with Aimee, and his wolf needed to know what it was. She might not be of his Pack, but she was close to one of his own.

But if he were honest with himself, he knew it was because of something more than that. She called to his wolf in a way he didn't quite understand. And it was something he knew he wanted to figure out.

He wasn't like his brothers or cousins. When they found their mates, it seemed to him that, other than his sister Brynn, each of them had fought the pairing. None of them had been in the right mindset to find mates, yet the moon goddess had blessed each of them.

Gideon had found his mate in Brie, a submissive wolf from another Pack. The two of them had carefully taken their steps down the path to mating to not only tighten their connections but also those between the Talons and the Redwoods. Brynn had been the one searching for her mate, and when she found it in Finn, she'd almost broken along the way. Ryder hadn't been looking for his fate when he found Leah, a water witch who had saved their den more than once. And Walker's fellow triplet, Brandon, had thought he'd not be long for his world but had ended up mating not one but *two* wolves—Parker and Avery.

As for Mitchell? Well, he too had fought the mating

bond for reasons of his own. But he had given in when he fell in love with Dawn. The moon goddess gave each of her wolves potential mates that they could find during their long lives. Sometimes, there was more than one, but the wolf *and* the human would decide if that person was their true fate. Walking away would hurt, a pain beyond agony, but sometimes, it was the only choice. Once the mating bond was made—a bite mark for the wolf, and sex for the human—none of the people involved would ever feel another potential mate as long as the mating bond stayed in place.

Walker had only heard of one mating bond being broken by anything but death, and he was pretty sure the terror that had come with that dark magic hadn't been truly worth it in the end.

Yet Walker, the one who was *ready* for a mate and wanted that connection, couldn't seem to find his. He'd been searching ever since Gideon became Alpha and their father's tyranny ended. He held back a shudder at that thought as he always did. His father had been a horrible man, a worse Alpha, and had truly scarred each and every one of his children to the point that it had shaped not only their lives and futures but also the way they found their mates.

But, no matter how many humans, witches, and wolves he met, Walker hadn't felt that tug, the pull that would tell him whether the other person was his mate.

Then Shane, a former human soldier who had been partially turned into a wolf thanks to a human torture experiment gone wrong, had been brought into the Pack, and mating bonds had changed yet again. Shane had been on the verge of dying and Gideon had been forced to make the decision to save his life. No one had known the ramifications of that act, but now Shane had two mates who would forever be thankful for what had happened, and the Pack had survived because they had a new member whose secrets had led them through the darkness.

Now, it was beyond difficult to tell who was your mate or not, and it took getting to know the person or persons as a human before the wolves were able to reveal who they *could* be. And even then, sometimes it didn't work. Each couple or triad was different, and finding the true path to mating didn't seem like it would get any easier anytime soon. Walker was afraid that some would lose out at finding their mate because there were so many obstacles.

He'd been happier when mating bonds were set in stone. Now, everything seemed so up in the air. Shifters had spent centuries finding their other halves one way and now having to find them another way meant that their world might forever be altered. It was shocking that *anyone* could find their mate.

Hence why this mating ceremony between Mitchell and Dawn was so important. This *proved* that mating bonds could still happen, even if it took a little more work. Dawn's eyes were bright, and Mitchell looked like a new man, a small smile playing on his lips as if he had a secret that only the woman standing in front of him knew. And as Mitchell bowed his head and took his mate's lips in a passionate kiss, Walker hoped that there was a way to find a potential mate that didn't end in pain and suffering.

Walker was a Healer, *the* Healer of the Talon Pack. It was his duty and honor to Heal those under his care from physical wounds, just as it was his triplet, Brandon's, responsibility as Omega to heal their emotional ones. Through his connection to the Pack, he was able to Heal injuries that were life-threatening, as well as simple cuts and scrapes. It physically hurt him *not* to use his energy and powers to help people.

And the idea that there were wolves—and now cats—out there who might be missing out on finding their mates because of a change to the Pack structure that wasn't their fault hurt him, as well.

"As Alpha, I bless this union as the moon goddess instructs me. I wish you both long, healthy lives as you find your true calling as mates." Gideon's deep growl ended on a howl, and Walker threw back his head, joining in on the song of his people.

The other wolves around him howled as well, and even the few witches who had been mated into the Pack and helped strengthen the wards joined in. The only three who didn't were the human women who had come with Dawn's brother and parents. Walker lowered his head and opened his eyes to watch them as they glanced around, laughter in their eyes. He had a feeling Dawn hadn't mentioned this part of the ceremony, but thankfully, none of them looked put off. If anything, they appeared as if they might have wanted to take part, but weren't sure how.

Given how much time they were spending with the Talons, they just might have their chance to find their places within the den wards at some point—even if they weren't Pack. There were a few humans in the Pack, but it was through special circumstance. In order to live as long as the wolves, they had to be changed. Only witches were able to truly tie their life forces to the Pack's without the change, though some of them did anyway. So, having these three humans within the den wards was...interesting.

And from the way they looked at Walker and his family, he had a feeling they thought it was interesting, as well. He wasn't like some of his family who heard the moon goddess's whispered words and spoke prophecy, but he had a feeling the lives of these women and his Pack would be forever entwined.

How that would happen, and what it would mean, he wasn't sure.

Kameron tugged on his arm, pulling him out of his thoughts, and he followed his triplet inside where the maternal females and submissives had set up a feast for everyone to celebrate Mitchell and Dawn's joining. He'd been tasked with setting up a few of the long tables, but he hadn't helped as much as the rest of his family since he'd been called away to help with a pup who had accidentally found a bush with thorns while chasing after a ball.

His family and Pack had welcomed Dawn in much smoother than some of the previous mates. Change was always hard, especially after their Pack had spent so long fighting for the right to exist, so he was glad the elders and the rest of the Pack had seemed to lighten up when it came to Dawn and her former Pack's past.

"I need to head out to do another run along the perimeter," Kameron said softly. "I'll swap shifts with one of the soldiers who couldn't come to the ceremony. That way, they can at least be part of the reception."

Walker nodded and picked up a cup of punch, handing it over to his brother before taking another for himself. Though their metabolisms as wolves worked much faster than humans', they could still get drunk after a while. And since Kameron was about to go on duty, and Walker was always on call as Healer, they'd stick to punch. He nodded to Leah, his brother Ryder's mate, and held up his cup. The water witch was his assistant in Healing, though her powers were much different than his. But, hopefully, she would understand that she could drink if she wanted to. However, since she had a young pup in her arms, he wasn't sure she'd want to indulge.

Their family had grown so much over the past few years, it was almost hard to keep up. But Walker would. Each and every member of his Pack and family were a part of him, soul deep, and he'd do anything to protect them.

Walker turned to his brother. "Anything I can do to help?"

Kameron shook his head. "We're on routine shifts right now since we're not sure who the fire witch was working for." He gave Kameron a look. Oh, they knew all right, but there wasn't anything they could do about it yet. Their new enemy was too good at keeping the blame off him and held far too much power.

Even working with the Redwoods, the Talons weren't strong enough to take on Blade and the Aspens yet. And even if they were, Walker wasn't sure it was the Aspens who were their new enemy, or just an Alpha gone rogue.

And for an Alpha to go rogue...well, that was something that could change everything.

Walker inhaled the sweet scent of a woman who made his wolf curious and turned as she stumbled into him. He caught her, pulling her soft body to his to keep her steady.

"You okay?" he grumbled, his voice lower than he'd intended.

"I'm fine. Just clumsy." Aimee pulled away, and he released her, aware that she was much weaker than he was, and he'd been taught not to let the humans realize that they weren't as strong as the wolves with everyday things.

"If you're sure." Kameron let out a sigh behind him, and Walker ignored his brother. He'd have to deal with the questions about his intense...whatever this was at some point.

"I'm fine," she repeated. "Thank you for catching me." She turned away then, going back to Dhani's side, and Walker did his best not to stare.

It wasn't only the Healer and wolf inside him that was drawn to this woman, but he wasn't sure if it was something *more*. His wolf wouldn't tell him if she was his mate or not, and with the new rules of mating that weren't actually rules at all, Walker wasn't sure he'd ever know.

But no matter where his mind went with potentials and fates, Walker knew one thing.

There was something wrong with Aimee.

And he was afraid there wouldn't be enough time with her on this Earth for him to find out what their connection was...or could be.

CHAPTER 2

AIMEE REAGAN HATED FEELING WEAK, yet the idea that she wasn't quite strong enough no matter how hard she tried seemed to be her forte these past few months. With a hand on the small of her back, she stretched, hoping the aching feeling would go away at some point. She'd been a waitress at the aged and rundown diner for a few years now, and she used to be able to make it further through a shift before she started to hurt. Her feet ached, her back bothered her even more, and her wrists throbbed from the weight of the trays she held. It wasn't anything uncommon for someone in food service, but she used to be able to last longer.

Heck, she'd been a waitress in some form or another from the time she was first able to get a job. At fourteen, she'd bussed tables as part of her high school courses, and as soon as she turned sixteen, she moved up to the hostess stand and sat people day in and day out. When she hit eighteen, she was finally able to waitress and had gotten a job at this very diner. They only served beer and boxed wine under their liquor license, but it was still a step up from most of the establishments around the country. She didn't work at a high-end place where she made hundreds of dollars a night, nor did she serve customers who sat at tables draped with white linen, but she made her way just fine.

It wasn't as if she had anything else to fall back on if she wanted out of food service. She hadn't been able to afford college, and her family was so in debt that it wasn't as if she could have asked them for a loan—even for community college. Her grades had been decent, but she hadn't excelled since her time was spent working towards helping her parents with rent and food instead of taking the AP classes she'd qualified for.

Aimee didn't hate her life or where she'd come from, but sometimes, she wished she could just catch a little break.

Her hands shook as she set them on the counter in the back galley, and she let out a slow breath. She had more bruises now than she had the day before and it was worrying. She'd gone to her doctor's small practice twice already this month and hadn't been able to get anything out of them except for some blood tests and a bill that had set her savings account back even more. No matter how much she paid monthly for medical insurance, it never seemed to be enough for her to qualify for anything except a blood draw and a shake of the head with a shrug when she asked what was wrong with her.

"*Nothing,*" they told her.

She just had thin blood and the aching muscles of someone twice her age. She was slowly wasting away, and her doctors had no answers for her, just more bills and fees.

And now that the dark circles under her eyes refused to fade away even under makeup, she had no more secrets either. Cheyenne, Dhani, and Dawn *knew* something was wrong with her, and she didn't have much longer until they cornered her and tried to get answers.

Only, Aimee didn't have any answers to give.

"Aimee, table seven needs more coffee," Traci said as she bustled by. "I'd fill them up, but you know how the boss is right now." She gave Aimee a look. "He's looking for any excuse to fire the old hires like us because we cost a couple of dollars more an hour."

Aimee sighed and reached out to grip her friend's elbow in a soft squeeze. "Thanks. I'll get right on it." Billy, their manager, had inherited the place from his father when he retired. Ali still owned the place and stopped by from time to time, but Billy was the one Aimee dealt with on a day-to-day basis.

And Billy *hated* spending money when he didn't want to, and if he could fire some of the older staff to save a penny, he would.

Not that Aimee was old since she was still in her twenties, but most of the staff here was high school students or early college age who didn't serve liquor. As soon as most of them hit twenty-one, they either graduated or moved on to higher-paying temp jobs.

Somehow, at the advanced age of twenty-five, Aimee had become one of the old ladies.

"Aimee, why the hell are you just standing there? I don't pay you to stand around playing with your phone." Billy glared at her, and she held back a sigh before picking up the coffee pot. She wasn't playing with her phone; she didn't even have it on her. She was on a tight plan and almost out of minutes since she'd spent so much time on the phone with her friends lately after Dawn's attack and everything that happened with that.

"On it," she said with a bright smile she knew probably looked a bit bitter.

"You better be." He stomped off after he growled, but she didn't flinch at his tone. After all, she'd spent time with *real* shifters who growled and snarled at the drop of a hat. A manager on a power trip didn't scare her. Yes, humans could be scarier than shifters most days since wolves never really hid what they were feeling, but Billy's growl didn't worry her.

She filled up table seven's coffees with a smile, then did the same with two other tables before going back to the galley where she set down the pot and let out a breath. She was *exhausted* and worried that she wouldn't be able to last much longer on her feet. It shouldn't matter though because she was almost done working for the day. She just had to get through this last hour.

Only, as she took a few steps, her vision blurred, and she gripped the edge of a chair to keep balanced. Bile filled her throat, and in the distance, she heard someone calling her name. She blinked a few times and tried to reach out again to break her fall. The floor rushed up at her, and a flaring pain shot up her wrist as she fell face-first over her arm and hit the ground.

People might have shouted or come to her, but she didn't sense any of them.

She didn't sense anything at all.

Only darkness.

Aimee opened her eyes to vivid pools of blue that called to her on a level she didn't quite understand. She blinked a couple of times, warmth filling her until the blue faded away and she instead found herself looking at the scruffy face of Walker.

Wait. Walker? Why was he at her diner? Was she still on the floor? She'd fallen, but maybe she'd hit her head and her dreams had brought in the one image that always soothed her even as it revved her up.

Not that she'd *ever* tell anyone that.

Walker couldn't be real, not right then. He barely felt tangible when she was awake and lucid. This must just be a weird dream. Soon, she'd wake up, embarrassed that she passed out at work. Because *that* much she remembered.

"You're in my dreams," she muttered, her voice thick with sleep, and her throat scratchy.

Those blue eyes came back into view, this time warmer. "You're not dreaming, Aimee, but why don't you wake up just a bit more for me so I can check out that head of yours."

Not quite what dream-Walker usually said to her. In fact, he didn't generally say anything at all since the two of them—in her mind anyway—were more often than not tangled around each other, heedless to any warnings her inner self might give.

As it turned out, she was thankful she didn't say any of that aloud. Because the more she blinked, the brighter the lights became around them, and she knew that, in fact, this was not dream-Walker. It was in-the-flesh-Walker, and she was on his medical bed.

Mortification set in, and she told herself it could be worse—she could have asked him to make out with her again or something equally as insane.

"What happened?" she asked.

"Why don't you tell us?" Cheyenne's voice came from her right, and Aimee tried to move to look, only to groan when her head spun.

"Okay, folks, let me check out my patient before you harass her," Walker grumbled.

"We're worried. We aren't harassing," Dhani put in.

"She's our friend." Dawn's voice was much stronger than it had been before, and for that, Aimee was grateful, but she was still worried about why all of them were there, and why she was in Walker's clinic to begin with and not in a human hospital.

"Drink this," Walker said, putting a cup to her mouth. She greedily drank down the water, letting it soothe her throat.

"Thank you."

He gave her a tight nod then went to look at the monitor above her bed. "You fell at work, that's all they would tell us. You've been unconscious for the past two hours. I don't think it was from hitting your head as your wrist took the brunt of the damage. It looks to be sheer exhaustion." His words were filled with anger at the end, and she wondered what she'd done to make him sound that way.

"Why am I here?" Aimee asked, afraid to look and see the worry on her friend's faces. She hated troubling them, hence why she'd tried to keep her illness—whatever it was —from them as long as she could.

"Don't you remember passing out at work?" Dhani asked.

"I...I remember that." She lowered her head to look down at her hands clasped in her lap. Walker had lifted the back of the bed so she could sit up, but she still felt out of sorts. She had a brace on her wrist, and it didn't hurt too badly, so she was grateful it wasn't a cast. But since it *didn't* hurt that much, she must have some form of drug in her thanks to the IV at her elbow. "But shouldn't I be in a human hospital?" She winced and looked over at Walker. "Sorry."

He shook his head. "Don't be. That would have been the case in most instances, but this was a special circumstance. I *am* medically trained, by the way. Have been for decades, and get recertified often. You don't need to worry on that account."

The word *decades* reminded her that he was far older than he looked and that her world wasn't the same as it had been before she learned about Dawn and the world of shifters and magic.

"Traci called me," Dawn said quickly. "Billy was just going to leave you there or some crap since he told everyone it was drugs and not a worker's comp thing. With the way the laws are right now given the new government regulations on wolves and witches, things are a little iffy in some areas, so he probably would have gotten away with it. Anyway, I came down with Mitchell, and we picked you up since we were only a block away. You didn't smell...off or too hurt, so we risked moving you. Plus, you woke up a few times so we knew you were fine for the most part, just tired and a little banged up."

Aimee didn't remember any of that. She could only recall the blue of Walker's eyes. Though Mitchell had similar ones, she knew Walker's by heart.

Cheyenne cleared her throat. "And this way, you won't have to pay as much." The other woman blushed, and Aimee wanted to crawl into a hole and die right then.

Of course, the others knew about her financial struggles, and before Dawn had mated Mitchell, she'd been in her own version of dire straits. But as much as she loved the fact that her friends cared more than her family seemed to these days, it still stung.

"I...see."

"No, you don't," Dhani said sharply. "Because none of

us see. It was a risk to bring you here, but Walker is a damned good doctor, and we knew you'd be in good hands."

"Thanks," Walker put in dryly, and Aimee had a feeling she wasn't the only one feeling out of sorts.

"But," Dhani continued as if Walker hadn't spoken, "we want to know *why*."

"I lost my job, didn't I?" Aimee put in, her mind catching up to what the others were saying. She knew they were trying to talk about something else, but she was a few steps behind and trying to figure out what the heck was going on. "That's why Billy mentioned drugs."

Dawn reached out and gripped her hand. "Yes, but don't worry. We'll find you something else. You already told us Billy is an asshole, but back to what Dhani was saying, honey. You've been keeping secrets, and I know I'm not one to talk, but we're here if you need us."

Aimee looked around at her friends and Walker and sighed. "I don't know what's wrong. No one knows what's wrong." She looked down at her hands. "But I'm dying."

Cheyenne and Dhani each cursed, while Dawn shook her head.

Walker was the only one who spoke aloud beyond those muttered curses. "Why do you say that?"

She met his gaze, her hands shaking. "Because I'm getting weaker, and they don't know why."

He frowned, his eyes not leaving hers. "Then we'll have to figure it out for ourselves, won't we?"

Aimee did her best not to let the promise in his voice allow a small kernel of hope grow within her. She'd wished all her life for things—stability, a roof over her head, a steady job, health—and she and her family had never been able to hold onto any of it.

It was as if she were truly cursed.

Dhani cleared her throat, and Aimee pulled her gaze from the wolf who hovered over her and looked over at her friend. "So, when Walker clears you, we'll take you to Dawn's house to rest for a bit."

Aimee frowned, ignoring the pulse in her temples that told her the pain meds were wearing off. "What time is it? Shouldn't you guys be at your jobs? I don't want to take you away from what you should be doing." She'd tried to hide how tired and worn she was over the past few months because each of her friends had other things in their lives that were important, and she hated pulling them away from them.

"It's after six," Cheyenne explained, running a hand down Aimee's cheek, a frown on her face. "I closed up early, and Dhani's done teaching for the day."

"And I work in the den now," Dawn put in. "The other maternals understood that I needed to be here." Dawn was a maternal, which she'd told Aimee was a wolf whose first imperative was to protect and care for children. She now worked at the daycare center in the den and cared for the children of the wolves on patrol or those who worked at any of the other small businesses within the den walls. Apparently, each den was pretty self-sufficient, something Aimee was only just learning, and a tidbit she wasn't sure many of the human population was even aware of.

Walker came up to her and deftly took out her IV so she didn't feel a thing. Since she knew he was decades older than she was, he had to have some practice at that. "You have a sprained wrist and a small cut on your forehead, but other than that, your fall didn't take much out of you. You should be able to move over to Dawn's when you feel up to it. As for what's going on *inside?* Well, that's something we'll just have to figure out together because, Aimee? I'm not letting it take you. Whatever it is, we're not letting it win. Understood?"

Aimee felt Cheyenne and Dhani stiffen beside her at Walker's tone, but it was the look on Dawn's face that worried Aimee. Her friend was looking at the Healer as if she'd just figured something out, yet Aimee had no idea what it could possibly be.

The only thing she knew was that she had no job, and that meant she might not be able to make her rent. But, in the end, she wasn't sure it would matter anyway because no matter how many words Walker used to try and comfort her, she knew the truth.

Whatever was wrong with her that the doctors couldn't find wasn't going away. And with each passing day, she got closer and closer to losing her battle. And though she had slowly started to come to terms with that over the past few months, when she stood by her friends and looked into the Healer's eyes, she knew she'd been lying to herself.

She had people to fight for, people to *live* for.

But she was afraid that no matter what she did, it would be too late.

CHAPTER 3

WALKER FROWNED at the leather-bound book in front of him before leaning back in his chair and pinching the bridge of his nose. Wolves didn't need glasses since their eyes self-corrected themselves thanks to their healing abilities, *and* Walker was able to fix anything their wolves couldn't, but right then, he saw double.

He'd spent too long going over old books that didn't tell him a damn thing when it came to the two things he searched for. He wanted to know more about mating bonds and their history to see if there was anything he could do to make them easier to sense. Things had been easier for potential mates before everything changed with the addition of a human-made shifter, and he was afraid that wolves were missing out on their futures because of it.

Short of going to the moon goddess and begging, he wasn't quite sure what he could do.

And though his siblings could hear the moon goddess's words, Walker had never been able to. The only time he'd ever come close was when he was having horrible nightmares over the course of Brandon's mating. His triplet had somehow been connected to the failing wards surrounding the den, and nightmares had plagued the three triplets. Kameron had been growly, not wanting to talk about it. While Brandon had leaned on his two new mates, Avery and Parker, to pull through.

Walker had written down every single dream he could remember so he could try and figure out what it all meant. In the end, they'd discovered that the three of them were reincarnations of the three original hunters who had been turned into shifters after the first hunter was blessed—or cursed if you wanted to think of it that way—by the moon goddess.

Their connection to the past had helped Brandon save his mates and restore the wards, and the nightmares that had plagued Walker ceased. Brandon had told Walker that the fact that they were reincarnations of the first set of shifters gave them stronger connections to their wolves. Knowing the magic and prophecy behind such a thing meant that they knew a part of themselves they hadn't before, but Walker wasn't sure it signified anything outside of the *knowing*.

Discovering where they'd come from was nice to know when he thought about the connection the three triplets shared with one another, but other than that, it was just another type of magic that was layered into his wolf and his Pack. The idea that his past incarnation had once been fully human didn't help him heal, but it did give him perspective.

Perspective that would hopefully help him find out more about the mating bonds and perhaps...perhaps save Aimee's life.

His wolf pushed against his skin at the thought, claws stabbing the edges of his fingertips. He wasn't such a dominant wolf that he constantly had control issues like some. He wasn't middle of the Pack either, nor was he a submissive. He was just a high-ranking wolf whose strength and control came from his Healing powers. The fact that his other half had become so aggressive just then to where he'd had to fight for control and keep from partially shifting at simply the thought of what was going on with Aimee told him something. It was more than just wanting to help a friend.

He had a feeling the issues he was researching might just be connected.

He let out a shuddering breath.

There was something about Aimee, and it wasn't just the way she made his wolf *feel*. He had to figure it out, and soon, if how she weakened right before his eyes was any indication. He was afraid if he weren't quick enough in discovering what he could do for her, she'd fade away completely.

His wolf growled, and he stood up from his desk, too agitated to study any more. Maybe he'd go for a run and let his wolf out so he could breathe again. He'd be able to center himself so he could find a way to help this human woman who meant so much to the newest member of his family.

A female who was beginning to matter in his life, as well.

He wasn't sure how it had happened, but he'd known from the moment he spotted her going through the wards at the nearest den when he was there to aid others in Healing, that there was something different about her.

Then she'd passed out going through the wards, and he'd caught her, bringing her close to his skin, her scent blending with his. She'd told him she was fine, that it must have just been a touch of lightheadedness, but now, he wasn't so sure. Hell, he hadn't been sure then either. Going though wards pulled on magic, that much was known. Humans with no connection to magic wouldn't feel a thing as they slid through the barrier. Cheyenne had walked through with permission from Dawn, who had been part of the Central Pack at the time and she hadn't felt anything beyond a prick of sensation along her skin— at least according to her. She'd remained upright and had rushed to Aimee's and Dhani's sides when the other two women hadn't faired so well.

Dhani had looked slightly lightheaded but had shrugged it off. He wasn't sure exactly what that meant, other than the fact that, for some reason, she was more sensitive to magic than most people—those like Cheyenne.

Aimee, on the other hand, had fallen into his arms. She'd obviously taken the brunt of whatever magic had slid through the wards and landed within her. At the time, his wolf had reached out, trying to Heal, but since she wasn't wolf *or* Pack, there hadn't been anything he could do.

And nothing had really changed in that regard since there was still nothing he could do for Aimee outside of human medicine, and she'd already exhausted most of their efforts before he was even aware that she was sick.

He growled low and forced himself to take a deep breath. He needed to run this energy off, or he'd end up growling at a pup or someone who didn't deserve it. In order to focus his talents as a Healer, he had to be the calm one, the seemingly laid-back one.

So he'd find a way to keep that façade now that Aimee was so close.

Aimee.

This sudden pull had to do with her, but he didn't know what it meant exactly. Was it because she was sick and his wolf *needed* to Heal? Or was it something more.

Perhaps it was a mix of both.

Instead of dwelling on something that would only fracture his control even more, he stripped off his shirt and toed off his shoes. He'd either shift here and go for a run in the surrounding woods, or he'd leave his jeans near a familiar tree. But the fabric of his shirt was a little too much on his sensitive skin at the moment.

He went back to mark where he was in his books just in case things got moved around since he was still at his clinic, and people could come in and out even though his office was off-limits. Once he'd done that, he headed out of his office, exited the clinic, and walked out into the paved area where people were still strolling since it was only early evening. He didn't have any patients, and if any came in, he'd feel them tug on his bonds as Healer, and Leah, his sister-in-law, who was a water witch and healer herself, could help. While he'd only been the Talon Pack

Healer for a little over three decades, he'd been through his share of wars and battles. He was glad to have the help, even in a time of peace.

That thought made him frown. Were they at peace? Everyone knew that Blade was up to something, along with either the entire Aspen Pack—or at least some of them—but Walker wasn't sure what their next move would be. It wasn't like with the Central War when they'd brought a demon to Earth and slowly pecked away at the Talon's allies and close friends, the Redwoods. And it wasn't like when Walker was younger, and they'd dealt with the totalitarian hierarchy of his father and uncles. Hell, even the war with the humans after the Unveiling where the secrets of shifters and witches had been revealed to the world was different than this. With the latter, they'd dealt with a frozen point in time when they were unsure how to proceed because wolves hadn't wanted to seem too aggressive and end up hurting more people in the end. However, with this, Walker wasn't sure any of them knew exactly what would happen next—only that *something was coming.*

Walker made his way to the forested area, nodding at shifters in both human and wolf form along the way as he thought about everything going on around them. He wasn't one to plan battles or even fight in them like his brothers and cousins. It had always been his job to stand on the front lines but to help those in need and aid those who fell. It was his job to care for his Pack and use every ounce of himself to make sure those that fell got up again. And because of that, his connection to his fellow Pack-mates of all dominance levels was slightly different than what the rest of his family had with them. He was the Pack's Healer, and that meant his people could *always* trust he would be there for them and that he wasn't at such a level that might intimidate. Every single wolf felt loved by their Alpha, Beta, Heir, Omega, and Enforcer, but there would always be a sense for some that they weren't truly comfortable alone with those in that hier-archy due to their power. Walker's magic was slightly... softer. So, as he walked past groups of people, they smiled easily at him and never once had to lower their eyes because of their wolves. That was how Healers worked, even if he didn't try.

Shaking off the odd thoughts that his mind tended to go toward, he made it to his favorite tree to shift behind and snorted when he saw that he wasn't the only one in need of a run tonight. Max and Kameron each leaned on different trees, their faces expressionless except for their eyes. Kameron looked curious with a touch of ice, while Max...well, Max just looked angry. That, however, wasn't anything new—at least since the accident—with how much his cousin seemed to hate the world.

They'd almost lost Max in the final battle with the humans after the Unveiling. And while his cousin might still be standing to tell the tale, he wasn't whole—physically or emotionally. His body still bore the scars on his torso and legs that may never fade away, even with Walker's Healing abilities, because when Max was hurt, his body had gone into shock. Max had also lost part of his right arm below the elbow and was still learning how to live again as a human *and* a wolf.

"Mind if I join you?" Walker said, his voice calmer than he felt.

Kameron unfolded his arms and stood straight. "We heard you coming, so we figured you'd join us." He narrowed his eyes at Walker. "You okay? You've had your head stuck in books most of the day, even when I came by to check on you."

Though Walker was the eldest triplet, Kameron had taken the role of older brother—the fact that the three of them were younger than all of their other siblings and cousins notwithstanding. That meant that Walker was used to the way Kameron constantly checked on them all. If they weren't near enough to each other to do a physical check, then Kameron would either call or tug on the Pack bond that his brother had as the Enforcer.

"I'm fine," Walker said quietly. "Just need to think a few things through, and a run should be good for me."

The others gave him a nod, and Walker wasn't surprised that Max hadn't said anything. It was rare for his cousin to speak these days after what had happened to him. Knowing all three had their own reasons for this run outside of the full moon, he stripped out of his pants and knelt down to begin his shift.

The familiar agony slipped through him as he tugged on the bond to his wolf. His bones broke and reformed, his muscles and limbs tightening and reshaping. Fur sprouted along his body, and soon, he was no longer man, but wolf. His human self was still at the forefront, his wolf half giving him time to get adjusted to his new body until it was time to run. Though with what Walker wanted to think about during the run, he might let his wolf hang back just a bit more than usual so he could focus.

The others were already shifted by the time he was done, and Walker did his best not to check on Max. It was taking time for Max to get used to running on three paws, and his cousin hated when Walker watched him as Healer to see if there was anything he could do. Shifters could heal most everything, but they couldn't regrow limbs.

They set out at a steady pace, Walker letting his wolf creep slowly to the forefront of his mind so he wouldn't have to worry about fallen branches and things to trip on. His senses were stronger in this form, his body more alert.

Max and Kameron trotted on either side of him, each of them running for their own reasons, while Walker let his mind wander. The pads of his paws pounded the ground as the three of them increased their pace, and he finally allowed his mind to turn to the problems at hand. The barest hint of the moon shone through the clouds, sliding over his fur, and he almost stumbled as his thoughts came together.

A curse.

That was what he felt whenever he was near Aimee. The taste of magic on the air when she came by, the overwhelming sense that something was *off* without any human medical reason for it.

He stopped where he was and knew the other two wolves around him would circle back in a moment. But Walker *knew*. He was now certain what was wrong with Aimee. As a Healer, once he could taste the magic, he *knew*.

How could he fix it? He had no idea. But now that he'd narrowed it down to a magical cause, he might be able to find a cure even though she wasn't connected to him through Pack bonds. If he had to, he'd find every witch he'd ever met and ask her if she knew how to save Aimee. Because she was important to Dawn, his new Packmate, and that meant she mattered.

That was the story he was telling himself anyway.

That, and the fact that he was a Healer and couldn't walk away from someone in need. There was no other reason for his desire to help her.

He had to find her, had to see her, to make sure he was right. Kameron and Max stood by him now, confusion obvious on their faces, but he turned to run back to his clothes. This was one of those times when Walker wished he could speak to others in his wolf form. The other two followed, and were soon shifting alongside him, all of them sweat-slick with their wolves in their eyes.

"What's going on?" Kameron asked, not bothering to pull on his pants. "Did you sense something?"

Walker shook his head and pulled up his jeans, too anxious to even finish buttoning them. "I think I figured out what's wrong with Aimee."

Max came out from behind the tree where he'd been changing in private since he didn't like to show off his scars and frowned, but he didn't say anything. Walker wasn't surprised.

Kameron narrowed his eyes and gave Walker a tight nod. "Go do your research or talk to her or whatever you need to do." His brother rolled his shoulders before bending to pick up his clothes. "I'm going for a run in human form if you need me." Since they'd all just changed back and forth so quickly in a short period of time, none of them would be shifting back to wolf form anytime soon without rest or food.

Walker nodded at the other two before running back toward the center of the den. He wasn't sure where he'd go first—Dawn's to see Aimee or to his office—but as soon as he came out of the clearing, his choice was made.

Aimee stood alone on the dirt path that led from the center of the den to the forest Walker had just moved from. Her arms were wrapped around herself, and she had a faraway look in her eyes as if she weren't really seeing anything in her field of vision.

She looked...lonely.

And his wolf pushed him to move forward, riding him harder than it had before. "Aimee." He hadn't meant for his voice to be a growl.

She jumped as she looked toward him and then glanced up since he was now right beside. No one else was around since they were all in different parts of the den or inside their homes. It was just the two of them.

Instead of telling her what he'd figured out or doing something smart like taking her inside so she didn't tire herself out, he leaned down and cupped her face.

"Aimee," he repeated.

"Walker?" she breathed, her lips parting.

And since his wolf pushed at him, needing something more than he could comprehend, he leaned down closer and kissed her. Just a soft brush of lips, barely a whisper of sensation, but a kiss nonetheless.

He pulled away, the surprise on her face matching his own at his actions. He hadn't meant to do that and wasn't quite sure why he had at all, but now there was no ignoring what he'd done.

But first, he had to tell her what he'd sensed because doing what he'd just done again was idiotic.

"What was that?" she asked, blinking quickly.

"That was my wolf." Her face went blank, and he could have kicked himself. "I was just looking for you." He truly wasn't saying the right things, but when he cleared his mind and got his head out of his ass, he'd apologize for handling all of this so poorly.

"Oh? What's wrong?" She took a step back, but he reached out and gripped her hand, stilling her.

"I think I figured out what's wrong with you."

She froze. "What do you mean?"

He let out a long breath. "It's not an illness, Aimee. You're not sick. You're cursed."

She didn't say anything, but the shock on her face was clear.

"And I'm going to do everything in my power to rid you of it. I'm not going to let this curse take you. Do you understand? It's not going to win."

And it wouldn't. Because he was a damn Healer and

he *knew* there was something in Aimee that called to him beyond his duty.

So he would figure it out, and he'd just have to pray he wasn't too late.

Because if he was? Well, that wasn't something he could think about.

CHAPTER 4

AIMEE SWAYED ON HER FEET, and Walker reached out, gripping her upper arms. The warmth of his skin penetrated the coldness that had seeped into her bones.

"Cursed," she repeated, her voice sounding oddly small. "Like...a curse-curse?" That question didn't make any sense, but then again, nothing did at the moment.

She couldn't quite keep up with everything that had happened in the last few moments, and considering that her life usually revolved around waiting on tables, that was saying something. One minute, she was outside of Dawn and Mitchell's, escaping the ever-diligent watch of the couple and her other two friends' care for a brief second so she could get fresh air; the next, she had Walker's mouth on hers; and yet the next...well, then he was speaking about curses and her illness as if he hadn't just made her sway on her feet for more than one reason.

Her lips tingled, and she could still taste him if she flicked out her tongue, but the thoughts of whatever had happened were fading so fast it was almost as if it were a dream.

Maybe she was now hitting the delusional part of her sickness because that seemed like the only logical reason at this point for what on earth had just happened.

Walker frowned before reaching out and running his knuckles along her cheek. She blinked, almost swaying into him, but she didn't say anything. She wasn't sure she could. There was this *connection* between them she couldn't name, and it was so strong, it almost overpowered everything else.

Even the most important thing.

Her *curse*.

She swallowed hard, pushing away the odd feeling that made her want to move closer to him and tried to catch her breath.

"I don't know what exactly made me think of it," Walker said softly, his gaze on hers. "I'm a Healer, and I needed to know what was wrong. Because, no matter what the doctors say, and what human science thinks, I knew something was wrong just as much as you did. But I couldn't think of what it could possibly be. I didn't want to force you to endure more tests and procedures to settle my brain, and that meant I needed to focus on what I *could* do. I needed to settle my wolf down, so I went for a run."

A *run* when it came to wolves didn't mean a jog in the park. No, it meant that he'd shifted into his wolf form and let his beast out. At least, that's what Mitchell had explained to her when he'd talked about his wolf. While she knew Dawn better than Mitchell, her best friend's mate had been a wolf for far longer and was also learning to open up to people who cared for his mate. Hence the fact that Aimee knew more about wolves from him rather than Dawn.

The run while in wolf form would also explain Walker's naked, sweaty chest. Once again, she swallowed hard and tried to keep her mind on task.

"And the run helped you figure out that I'm cursed?" How on earth had she become this person who could talk about these things so easily? Curses and wolves, and being held by half-naked men that made her body ache. This was her new normal, and she wasn't sure she was quite equipped to deal with it.

"It let my wolf come closer to the surface so I could *think*. And because I'm a Healer, or maybe because—" He cut himself off and shook his head. He gave her a strange look as if he wanted to tell her something else that had nothing to do with being a Healer but couldn't. Or perhaps...wouldn't. And a small part of her *needed* to know what that was. "I don't know why it took me so longer to figure it out, but I *know* it's a curse now. We both know it's not truly medical and nothing human. And you *are* human, so it's not a connection to the moon goddess or something wrong with your powers or being a wolf." He paused. "Because you aren't one. But I'm going to figure it out, Aimee. I'm not going to let whoever did this to you get away with it." He growled the last part, and his eyes glowed gold.

She almost took a step back at the intensity of it but stopped herself.

"You're saying someone set a curse on me, and that's why...that's why I'm dying?" It wasn't easy to say the words aloud, but she knew the truth. She'd known for some time now.

Walker let out a growl, and she froze. She'd heard the others in the Pack growl, of course, and had met many of Dawn's former Packmates, as well, but she wasn't sure she'd ever heard Walker growl. He was so laid-back most of the time, that it was hard to remember he had a wolf lurking beneath his skin.

There was no hiding it now.

"We're not going to let that happen. *I'm* not going to let it happen."

If there were a way to truly trust the promise in a vow like that, she would. But she knew that even if he was right about the curse, there was no guarantee that they would be able to fix it. No one had been successful in helping her *at all* so far. In fact, most of the doctors she'd seen in the past had thought she'd been faking her issues rather than looking beyond the surface. It wasn't as if they knew about curses and the mythical.

"Aimee? What's wrong?" Dawn ran up from behind her, Cheyenne and Dhani on her tail.

Her three friends couldn't be more different yet, at the same time, she saw their similarities in the way they were connected to each other—Aimee included. Before they found out that Dawn had been born a wolf, Aimee had thought her friend more similar to her than the other two. And in some ways, that was still the case as the two of them weren't as outspoken as their friends. But Dawn had always had a slight edge to her, a protectiveness that came out when they least expected it. Aimee would have liked to think she had something similar, but nothing she had compared to a wolf. Dhani could be as soft as Aimee but had a temper that rose out of nowhere sometimes when it came to any perceived injustice. And Cheyenne was fiercer than the three of them combined—and she wasn't a wolf.

They'd each come together slowly in such mundane

circumstances that Aimee wasn't even sure how they'd become the fearsome foursome they were. It was as if they'd *always* been a tight unit. And though each of them held their own private lives and secrets because everyone needed that, she knew she could trust them completely. Hence why she'd *finally* told them about what might be ending her life. And why she would now tell them what Walker had just told her—vague as it was.

Dawn cupped her face, and Aimee blinked. "What is it? Aimee?"

She'd been lost in her thoughts again and had worried everyone. Again. She needed to stop doing that. Of course, as soon as she thought that, a wave of nausea swept over her and she swayed.

Walker had his arms around her from behind in an instant, eliciting strange looks from the other women as he pulled her close.

"Do I need to take you back to the clinic?" he asked, his face close to hers once again after he rotated her in his arms. His hold was so strong yet gentle, and the warmth radiating from his bare skin seeped into her bones, giving her the strength to pull away so she didn't make a fool of herself once again at the most inappropriate time.

"I'm fine," she said softly then shook her head. "Well, not *fine,* clearly, since I'm here for a reason, but it was just a little nausea." Her face heated since she hadn't meant to mention that to Walker, but he was a Healer and had probably heard and seen worse.

Dawn pulled her closer while Cheyenne and Dhani hovered nearby. "Let's get you back inside at least, then we can talk." Her friend looked over at Walker and frowned like she wanted to say something else but wasn't sure what. Aimee wasn't sure there was much to say at all at this point.

Walker stuffed his hands into his pockets and rocked back on his heels. "I'm going to get the rest of my clothes and do some more research. I'll let you all talk about what I just said, but I'll be back soon." He met Aimee's gaze again, and she barely stopped from sucking in a breath. He always did that to her, and she wasn't quite sure how she felt about it. "I'm sorry I dropped this on you, I didn't mean to. I'd planned to have notes and an actual plan rather than just blurting it out."

Dhani snorted as she pulled Aimee closer. Apparently, today was tug-on-Aimee day. "Yes, making someone panic by saying things like *curse* and *magic* isn't the best way to go about things. I know this might be a hard thing for you shifters to understand, but us humans need a little lead time to get used to this whole paranormal thing."

Aimee winced at Dhani's tone, but Walker didn't seem to mind. He just gave them a nod before leaving the four of them standing in the middle of the path, Aimee's mind still whirling. She wasn't exactly sure what had just happened, but she had a feeling something big was coming.

Of course, since finding out that Dawn is a shifter, something big always seemed to be on the horizon.

"What the hell was that?" Cheyenne asked as soon as Walker was out of earshot—or at least Aimee hoped he was considering he was a wolf with enhanced senses.

"I have no earthly idea," Dawn said slowly, but I think we should all go inside and sit down before we try and figure it out."

"Tequila would probably help," Dhani mumbled.

"Lots of tequila would probably be better," Aimee agreed, not looking at the women around her. Instead, her attention was focused on the direction Walker had headed. What the hell was wrong with her? Why couldn't she concentrate on anything that was important?

Soon, she once again found herself in Dawn's home; this time, trying to explain what Walker had told her only a few moments before—though it wasn't as if he'd said much. If anything, he'd only confused her more by saying anything at all.

"That's it? He got all wishy-washy about being a Healer and said you were cursed?" Cheyenne frowned before starting at Dawn. "Is that how this whole Pack thing works? The wolves rely on magic and...poof, there's a premonition, and that answers everything?"

As Cheyenne had a very analytical mind, her words didn't surprise Aimee in the slightest. Dawn, however, put her hands over her face and let out a small growl. Since the sound came out more wolf-like than human, it surprised Aimee for a moment but, hopefully, she hadn't let the surprise show.

"I have no idea what he was thinking, or why he even said it at all without proof or something beyond whatever the hell he just did, but what I can tell you is that Walker wouldn't have said something at all if he didn't think it was true. I might not know my new Healer and family member as well as I'm learning some of the other Brentwoods, but I know that much about the man." Dawn looked up at Aimee and met her gaze. "So, if he thinks you have a curse on you? Then, maybe, just maybe, he's right."

Cheyenne and Dhani each mumbled something but Aimee just stared at Dawn, trying to get her mind to work. She was already exhausted beyond measure and trying to get a grip on the fact that she'd passed out recently and lost her job. And of course...there was the kiss. *That* kiss. It had come out of the blue and *far* surpassed anything she could have ever dreamed of, and yet she had no idea what it meant or if it meant anything at all.

She wasn't sure she could take much more.

But she didn't have a choice.

She never did.

"So...a curse." Aimee said, taking a deep breath. "This is straight out of science fiction, you guys."

"More like horror," Dhani said with a shrug. "What? It's true."

"Okay, so I'm apparently living in my own horror novel," Aimee said dryly. "What the hell do I do about it?"

Dawn frowned. "I have no freakin' idea. I'm new to the whole Pack thing and never really met any witches so I don't know how curses work."

"So, witches are the ones who do the curses?" Aimee asked. "Why on *earth* would a witch curse me?" And how long did she have if the curse was truly real? Her stomach rolled, and her skin went clammy. She wasn't sure if that was from the so-called curse itself or just thinking about it.

"I don't know, but you're not alone in this," Cheyenne said before swearing under her breath. "We need to go, Dhani. You have that meeting, and I have work to do at home since I'm on call. We're only a phone call away though, damn it."

Aimee hugged her friends, forcing herself to be stronger than she felt. She'd always had to rely on her own type of strength to get through her childhood and the fact that her family constantly fell into times of despair, but this was something altogether different.

"I hate not knowing things. I hate not having answers." Aimee stood and paced in Dawn's living room, not sure if she should leave and go home, or stay longer. It wasn't as if she had anywhere else to go at the moment, and for some reason, she had a feeling if she left, things would only get worse.

"I'm with you," Dawn said before standing. "And since Walker is now coming toward the house, maybe we'll get a few answers from him."

Aimee turned toward the door, her pulse racing. Dawn gave her a look and, once again, Aimee cursed shifter senses. Hopefully, her friend would think her reaction had more to do with the subject matter and less to do with the man about to enter the house. As it was, it was already a mix of both.

When the door opened, Mitchell and Walker stood on the other side, though why Mitchell had knocked on his own door was only apparent when Aimee realized that Walker was blocking the way.

Walker wore a shirt this time, and she told herself she was not disappointed that she couldn't see his bare chest and arms anymore. Her heart raced, and she didn't think it was only because of what he might be here to say. Why couldn't she control her reactions when it came to him?

He held a book in his hand she hadn't noticed at first,

and as Mitchell pushed his way into the house behind him, Aimee only had eyes for Walker.

"I wanted to apologize again for blurting out my thoughts the way I did," Walker said softly, and though he was talking to the entire room, he was focused on her. She wasn't sure how she felt about that, nor would she know how she'd have felt if he looked the other way.

"It's fine," she said, knowing her words were honest ones. She wasn't sure if wolves could taste a lie like they could in books, but she wasn't going to start lying when it seemed that her life was on the line. "There's no easy way to say that." Or any way at all, really.

"I'm not a witch, nor do I know if it was a witch who did this to you," Walker continued, ignoring the others in the room. The girls paced around him while Mitchell studied his cousin, but Aimee only saw all of this out of the corner of her eye. She wasn't sure what Walker noticed, but he was a shifter, and probably saw a lot more than she did.

"A lot of things can cause curses," Mitchell added. "Though witches are the ones who usually do it," he said, echoing his mate's words.

"All I know is that I *know*." Walker let out a growl before visibly slowing his breathing. "And I hate this magic crap that gives me no words, no guidance." He held out the book with a torn leather spine and frowned at it. "I can read about what might be harming you, but I don't know if I'll be able to do anything about it. I'll talk to Leah and the other witches, but they might not know either. I'm a Healer, but I can only Heal Pack." He looked at her as if he were trying to convey something she couldn't understand. "Humans can't enter the Pack," he said slowly, and Mitchell cursed.

"They can if they're mates, but they have to be changed soon after," Mitchell growled. And before Aimee could react to anything either of them had just said, her friend's mate continued, "I've heard of a couple of humans being allowed into a Pack without mating bonds, but it's not a proven thing. Hell, Gideon could slice your hand right now and try to form a Pack bond, but that doesn't mean the moon goddess will grant it."

Aimee held her hand up. "Wait, what on earth are you talking about? You're like ten steps ahead of me here, and I hate feeling like I'm always trying to catch up."

"What they're saying is that Walker thinks the only way to Heal you is if you're Pack, and the only way to *become* Pack, is to no longer be human, am I on the right track?" Dawn asked, her eyes going gold.

Aimee knew enough about her friend to know that meant that Dawn's wolf was now at the surface. Suddenly, the reality of her new circumstances settled in, and she almost had to sit down. She was in a room with three shifters who were talking about her humanity and curses from witches as if it were a regular occurrence. At some point, she'd like to get off the wild train from Hell and find a way back to sanity again.

"That's an option," Walker said. "We need to talk to the witches. We need to figure this out. Because you smell of magic, and I'll be damned if I let whoever did this to you win."

There was such sincerity in his voice that she almost lost the words' meaning at first.

She smelled of magic?

She was only a human. A now-former waitress with a friend who happened to be a wolf. She wasn't anyone special.

She was just a dying mortal.

But from the look in his eyes, Aimee had a feeling that all of that was now in her past. She only had to take a deep breath and figure out the next step.

When she did, however, she hoped she was strong enough to find her way when the dust settled.

CHOICE

BLADE HAD ONE CHOICE, one chance, really. He knew what must be done to ensure his role and keep his plans on the right track, he just hated that he had to do it at all. No, he didn't care that someone had to die to make sure his plans came to fruition, but he did hate the fact that he had to take such a risk this early in the game.

Annoyed that he had to go to these extremes at this stage, he let out a growl that would have startled most mortals.

The red witch in front of him wasn't most people, nor was she truly mortal anymore. She'd mated into his Pack after all, and because of that, she had the perk of a longer life than most of her kind could ever even dream of.

It took great sacrifice for a witch to live past her mortal years if she couldn't find her mate within a shifter Pack, and Scarlett, Blade's personal fire witch, had found hers years ago. At least, that's what Blade had always been led to believe. He didn't think a witch could *force* a mating to find immortality, but then again, mating bonds weren't something he really cared about too much.

He'd had his mate once—just long enough to have his son, Chase—and when he lost her in one of his prior battles, he'd grieved in his own way. After all, that meant he couldn't have any more of his progeny out in the world since, in order for shifters to have children, they had to be mated first.

He'd at least shown grief to those who mattered, and they had rallied around him, securing his place as the beloved Alpha of the Aspen Pack. Those under him had gathered together to give him their strength—at least most of them.

His Beta, Audrey, a lion shifter with an attitude, was starting to ping his radar, and he had a feeling she would soon become more trouble than she was worth. As long as she didn't get in the way of his ultimate plans, she'd survive. But if she did? Well, it looked as if he might need a new Beta soon.

"Are you almost done?" Blade asked, stalking towards his witch.

Scarlett looked up from her cauldron—because, apparently, a bowl would be too mundane for this witch—

and raised a brow. "Magic takes time, Blade. You know this. If you want me to do your dirty work, stop breathing down my neck. It's unbecoming."

He flipped her off, but she just rolled her eyes and got back to work. She'd been dealing with this spell for a few hours now, and he was already tired of it. He needed it to work so he could move on to the next phase of his plan.

In order for him to become Supreme Alpha—the Alpha of all Alphas and a title not yet bestowed upon a wolf in this day—he needed to have the loyalty of *all* of the Packs in the United States and, ultimately, the world. Right now, however, that allegiance seemed to be with his rivals—the Talons and Redwoods. Both of those Packs had caused so much disaster and terror within the past thirty years with their wars and the Unveiling, yet the other Packs looked up to them for guidance and lauded them for the way "*they took care of it.*"

Blade barely held back a snort. All they did was create more uncertainty for all the Packs, but did anyone see that but him? No.

Who had been the one to protect his Pack from all prying eyes over time—human or wolf? Him.

Who had been the one to ensure the secrecy of cat shifter even within the wolf shifter den and mythology? Him.

Who had kept his *other* secrets from the others? Him.

After all, until recently, *no one* but his Pack knew that shifters could also be cats, but he had a feeling that was out of the bag thanks to the meddling Beta below him.

Blade needed power and respect, and in order to get that, he needed *all* of the Packs to look to *him* for guidance, not the Talons or Redwoods. The problem with that plan at the moment was that there was only *one* wolf connecting them all through treaties and understandings.

And it wasn't an Alpha.

No, it was the Voice of the Wolves who had visited each and every Pack around the globe to ensure that they were all connected to the Talon Alpha instead of Blade.

So, Blade would use his witch to take out the Voice of the Wolves and step into that role when it was time.

No one would miss Parker, not when Blade's witch was done with him.

Parker was a son of the Redwoods, but he was now a Talon. Take him out, hurt the Pack, leave a hole for Blade to step into.

The plan was perfect.

And from the grin on Scarlett's face, it was time to put it into action.

Finally.

CHAPTER 5

WALKER HAD SERIOUSLY GONE off the deep end. He wasn't able to communicate, and he only had his lack of sleep—and his dick—to blame. If he hadn't been so head over heels in...whatever the fuck he was with Aimee, maybe he could have formed a rational sentence. As it was, he felt as if he were going full-pace twenty steps ahead, when they should be back at the starting line trying to figure out what the next step *was*.

Throughout it all, though, he had to wonder, was she his mate?

Was *that* why he was acting this way? Or was it because of his call as Healer?

The latter seemed like a cop-out, but the former wasn't a guarantee, not with the changes in the mating bonds—the other part of the puzzle he'd been trying to figure out.

Annoyed with himself for letting his mind wander again, he stripped off his clothes and stepped into the shower. He hadn't bothered to put on pajamas the night before or even sleep in his boxers since he'd, once again, slept at his desk, trying to research how the hell to help Aimee. Now, his body not only hurt, it also didn't smell the best.

Not the greatest way to meet the woman constantly on his mind.

He let the hot water slide over him and his aching muscles as he thought about Aimee and what she could be to him. This wasn't the first time she'd been on his mind when he was thinking about mates, and he had a feeling it wouldn't be the last. She called to his wolf like no other, and though he didn't have that automatic feeling that told him a mating bond could happen, he *knew,* just like he *knew* about the curse. There was something special about her.

But before he could do anything about it and discover what his feelings might be, he had to erase the dark circles under her eyes and the fear within their depths.

He couldn't lose her, not when he'd potentially just found her.

And even if she weren't his mate, he couldn't lose her.

He *liked* her, and she deserved far better than the hand she'd been dealt. Once he found a way to Heal her, she'd be whole again, and then he could see if she were truly his mate.

Because, like he said, though he couldn't seem to carry on a coherent conversation when it came to her, he couldn't stop wanting her.

Hence his complicated mindset at the moment.

With a sigh, he quickly finished his shower before toweling off and figuring out what he was going to do with his day. His infirmary was, thankfully, empty, and he didn't have any appointments today. There were a couple of pregnant wolves in the den, and he'd find a way to check on them without making them feel like they needed him to, but other than that, he had the whole day to do research.

And talk to Aimee.

He couldn't help himself. There was this need to be in her presence that went far beyond that of a Healer, and that meant he would have to do what he could just to be near her. After throwing on whatever clothes were handy, he rolled back his shoulders and headed toward Mitchell and Dawn's. Though Aimee had an apartment in town, they'd all convinced her to stay within the den for the night so their wolves could settle.

Most of them were so dominant, they'd never be able

to let a weaker person in their care out of their sight without doing something to protect them. While Walker wasn't as dominant as Mitchell or even Dawn, he felt the same as they did about Aimee's wellbeing.

Well, maybe not exactly the same, but that was something he and Aimee would have to discuss. For all that he'd desired a mate in the past, Walker honestly had no idea what the next step was in actually figuring it all out, especially when the other person wasn't a wolf. Most of his brothers had mated wolves who felt—or would have felt—the tug just like they did, and the others had special circumstances that led to their mating. Only his sister, Brynn, had been through the horror of finding out her mate felt *nothing* when it came to a mating bond until it was nearly too late. Everything had worked out for her and her mate, Finn, but it had almost cost the two of them too much.

Walker wasn't sure he'd be able to handle it if what happened to Finn happened to Aimee, but since the woman on his mind was already sick, and he was helpless to do anything about it, he knew things might only get worse before they got better.

Before he could head to Aimee, however, he had to deal with the wolf on his porch. His brother and Alpha, Gideon, had arrived about five minutes earlier and had just taken a seat in the rocking chair instead of coming inside. That meant that his brother had things on his mind but wasn't in too much of a hurry. Either that, or he knew Walker would be right out. Though Gideon wasn't a foreseer like their sister-in-law, Avery, his brother's sense of what was coming was sometimes uncanny. Walker supposed that was what happened when one was connected to each and every member of the Pack at such a deep and visceral level.

"Did you want coffee?" Walker asked as he stood in his open doorway.

Gideon shook his head. "I had some with Brie earlier. She and Fallon are headed to the nursery early today, so I had a little time this morning to chat."

Walker held back a wince at the emphasis on the word *chat* before taking a seat in the rocking chair next to Gideon's. "What did I do?"

His Alpha sighed. "Nothing, you honestly haven't done a single thing, and I'm not sure why I'm even here other than to lend support or be an ear if you need it."

Walker didn't say anything, knowing his brother would let him know what was on his mind eventually.

"I don't know what we can do, Walker." Gideon's voice was low, his wolf quietly on edge but not fully at the forefront yet. "You know the new rules that came into effect when we made the treaty with the humans. We can't make new wolves right now, not with so many eyes on us. After what happened to Avery on camera and how she was forced into changing...the humans are watching us so damn closely, it could do more harm than good. For everyone. There's really no protocol right now for what happens if we change a human to a wolf, but if the humans find out, they could take Aimee away from us. Or start another all-out war."

The wolf was fully in Gideon's voice now, and Walker couldn't blame him. The wolves and humans had only been at tentative peace for a little over a year now, and one of the more recent concessions was that no more humans could be turned into shifters...unless they were mates of the wolves.

And the latter part wasn't something understood by the humans enough for anyone to know what would happen if someone *was* turned. Walker knew Gideon hadn't agreed to the rule, and no other Alpha had either, but they hadn't been able to shut it down completely either, not when they were trying to keep the peace. Hence why it was a *rule* and not a *law*.

"Is she your mate?" Gideon asked, his voice soft now, though still rough with his wolf.

"I don't know." Walker paused, his wolf pressing him to continue. "You know the mating bonds aren't the same as they were even a year ago." Gideon nodded. "What if she's not my mate? What if this is just attraction, and I tell her that it could be a mating? Not only would I be hurting her unnecessarily, I could be giving her hope that maybe our potential mating bond could save her. I don't know if I can do that to her."

They were silent for a little while longer before Gideon stood up, his attention on the horizon and the rising sun through the trees instead of Walker.

"We're going to fix the mating bonds," Gideon said after a moment. "I *know* it. Our wolves can't continue to live this way, in the unknown. It's not healthy for the Pack. And I know it's my fault the bonds are screwed up because I changed the blood bonds of the Pack in order to save another, but we're going to find a way to change it back."

Walker hoped that was the case; after all, when he wasn't focusing on Aimee's curse, he was looking into past archives to see if this had ever happened before. Wolves were so long-lived that it was a possibility that the mating bonds had been changed in a previous lifetime.

"Don't hide who you are or what you could be," Gideon continued. "I did that once and almost lost everything. It may be that neither of you has anything to lose by trying. Tell her what's on your mind, Walker. I have a feeling she might already know more than you think." And with that cryptic comment, his Alpha walked away, leaving Walker alone with his thoughts for a few long moments.

"Stop being a coward," he whispered to himself.

His wolf growled in agreement.

When he found himself at Mitchell and Dawn's door, it was Aimee who answered. She had dark circles under her eyes, and he swore she'd lost more weight overnight, but she still gave him a tentative smile when she saw him. She also rolled back her shoulders and showed the inner strength and grace he'd come to admire in the time he'd gotten to know her.

"Dawn said it was you at the door so I should answer," Aimee said by way of greeting. "That whole sense of smell thing gets a bit weird after a while, no?"

Walker smiled, his body relaxing at the sound of her soothing voice. "I'd say you get used to it, but even after all these years, I have days where I'd rather not have my presence announced so quickly."

She met his gaze and smiled again. "What do you say we go for a walk? I know you're here to talk, and I could use some air. Plus, apparently, having a conversation with wolves around means there's no such thing as privacy."

Walker held out a hand, hoping he was doing the right thing. "I think that sounds like a good idea. And you're right, there's never any privacy when you're surrounded by wolves."

Especially if they're his well-meaning family.

He took her through the wards to the neutral territory right outside the den. They weren't at war anymore, and no one was forced to stay inside the boundaries any longer. There were still sentries and guards on duty at all times, but there wasn't the sense of impending danger that there had been for so long after the Unveiling when the humans were at war with the wolves.

"It smells so clean out here," Aimee said. "You could almost forget that there's a major city not too far away, you know?"

Walker nodded. "That's why the Pack bought all this land centuries ago. No matter how much money some companies throw at us, they can't buy our commitment to what keeps us sane. It's our home."

"It's beautiful."

It wasn't until they were getting close to where a few of the other wolves were training outside the wards that Walker realized he was still holding Aimee's hand.

He didn't let go, but he knew he should probably talk about what he'd planned to instead of chatting about the den, the weather, and other inane things. Especially since it only spoke of some of their personalities rather than whom they truly were.

"What did you want to talk about, Walker?" Aimee asked, pulling him to a stop just out of hearing distance of the wolves in the training ring.

Walker spotted Brandon, Parker, and Avery among those present and gave them a slight nod before turning back to Aimee. The triad was training together with a few other wolves, and Walker was glad to see them out like this. They were still a newly mated triad, even so many months in, and they didn't have much time with one another given all three of their positions in the Pack. Avery was also one of the newer wolves, so she needed more training than most of them. Thankfully, she had Parker and Brandon to help her, as well as the rest of the Brentwoods.

"There're a lot of things we should talk about, but every time I try to say something to you, I feel like I'm making a fool of myself."

She gave him a weird look. "That's how I feel, too. Not that you're making a fool of yourself, but that I'm the one being an idiot. It's like I've never had a conversation with another person before. When I'm around you, my mind seems to go on the fritz, and I forget how to put words together in a coherent sentence."

"You sound plenty coherent now." He ran his thumb along the side of her hand, his wolf in agreement with the man—they needed to know more about Aimee.

She snorted, her nose scrunching up in an adorable way that brightened her eyes and made the dark circles underneath practically melt away. If he had any say, that darkness would never come back. He'd made this vow not only because he was a Healer, but because she was *his*. And when he was able to voice the words, he would say them aloud, as well. She needed to hear them, and he needed to feel the connection to her when he said it.

"That's only because we're alone...ish." She gestured toward the others around them just out of earshot. "Which makes no sense since it used to be the opposite."

He turned to her, cupping her face, though he knew he should slow down so he could get his thoughts in order. But the mating heat—and damn it, it *had* to be the mating heat—rode him hard, and he could only fall into its sweet embrace.

"I need to kiss you," he whispered, thinking he must be losing his mind.

Her eyes widened. "I need that, too. But we also need to talk...right? I mean, this is crazy. There are a million things more important than what I need from you right now, yet this is the only thing I can think about. It makes me feel like I'm making stupid and selfish decisions but... I don't care."

He slid a strand of her hair behind her ear and frowned. "Talking...talking we're going to do. I promise you. But never think that doing something for *yourself* is selfish when all I've known you to do is things for others." He licked his lips, his eyes on hers. "And, by the way, you were pretty coherent there, too."

He lowered his head, his lips a mere breath away from hers. He knew he was moving too fast; something so unlike him, it was as if something else were pushing him to act like this. There were people around, watching, and he was normally such a private person, he'd have never held someone so close like this before.

But this was Aimee, and there was something about her that drove him in a new direction.

Heat spread over Walker's face, but he knew it didn't come from the woman in his arms. He looked up, only to growl and pull Aimee closer to him. He hit the ground with her tucked into him, seemingly trusting him completely with her safety, and rolled over her as the fire swept over them, licking and flicking its heated tongues over his skin before continuing on to its intended target.

Someone screamed, and fire slammed through the trees from four directions, one large stream burning over Walker's and Aimee's heads.

"Witch," Walker rasped, and Aimee tugged his arm down so she could see, though he still did his best to cover her and shield her from the worst of it. He was a wolf and could heal. He knew she didn't have much time as it was, human or not.

"What's going on?" Aimee asked from beneath him. "Where did all this fire come from? Are you hurt?"

He shook his head and opened his mouth to say something, but as quickly as the fire had appeared, it dissipated just as fast.

Leaving only destruction and a pained howl in its wake.

"Parker!" Brandon yelled, and Walker was on his feet so fast, he barely had time to blink.

Only the need to keep Aimee safe made him slow down so she could run by his side toward where his brother-in-law lay on the ground between his two mates. Other soldiers and wolves ran around them, seeking out those who would harm their Pack, and Walker knew Kameron's men would be on the prowl soon.

But Walker wasn't a soldier.

He was a Healer.

He didn't run toward the attackers.

He ran toward the fallen, heedless of claws, magic, and bullets. That was his duty to his people, his Pack, his family, and his moon goddess.

A responsibility he had never forsaken.

Never taken lightly.

He went to his knees at Parker's side and was vaguely

aware that Aimee had kept up with his long strides. Now, she stood behind him, her hand on his shoulder yet still out of the way so others could move around and she wouldn't end up in the line of fire. The way they'd moved together had been instinctual to both of them, and he would have to think about the *why* of that once he did what he had to do.

He didn't have time to think about who the fallen was or the fact that his brother would never be the same if Walker weren't fast enough. He couldn't think about the fact that Parker was one of the good ones, and that he had already sacrificed himself and his future once before to save them all. He couldn't think about the fact that this man was not only family through mating but also a friend that Walker counted on.

He couldn't think about the fact that if he couldn't save him, they would not only be in a full-scale war with whoever had done this, they could go into it in a blind rage that could cost more lives than if they had time to plan.

He couldn't think about any of it.

He could only concentrate on the wounds that marred Parker's flesh, and the agony ripping through his veins. That was what called to his wolf, and it was what Walker could use to get him through the painful process to come.

"What the fuck happened?" his triplet, Brandon

barked. Though they weren't identical, he knew the rage in Brandon's eyes matched his own.

At least, on one level.

The utter agony beneath the rage was one of a mated pair and triad that Walker didn't understand...yet.

"It was a witch," Walker bit out, then looked down at Parker, holding his reaction to what lay before him deep inside. It wouldn't do anyone any good for him to reveal what he felt at this point.

Parker's flesh had been seared in some places, crisped in others. Bruises marred the parts of his skin that weren't burnt, and Walker had a feeling the other man had thrown himself on top of one of his mates when the fire came close and there was nowhere to run. No one else's flesh held a true burn mark.

Only Parker's.

His clothes were mostly ash at this point, yet the wolf had his eyes open and locked on Avery. Walker knew if Brandon had been closer to Parker's head, it would have been his other mate he looked at. But for now, she was his touchstone, and Walker would use that.

"Do we need Leah?" Brandon asked.

Walker nodded but wasn't sure there was time to get their sister-in-law. Leah was a water witch, a healer—the antithesis of the fire witch that had thrown flames Parker's way with such precision. It could have only been because of a dark curse.

Someone must have taken out his or her phone to call Leah, but he couldn't focus on that. No, his attention could only be on the man below him. Walker closed his eyes and tugged on the cord that connected him to his wolf and Healing powers. Each Healer—like any of the named hierarchy within the Pack—had a bond with each and every Pack member. Some were stronger than others, but his new one with Parker since the man had recently joined the Talons after his mating with Brandon and Avery was *strong*.

Because Parker was damned strong.

And so was Walker.

His warmth slid through him and out of his fingertips, heading down the bond that connected him to Parker. The other wolf's chest rose and fell as he shook, but Walker didn't let up. He Healed. It hurt. It wasn't easy, not this time, but he didn't stop. Would never stop. The triad had been through enough in their lives, and he'd be damned if he let a witch do anything more to them.

Every time Aimee squeezed his shoulder, he felt stronger. He didn't know if it was in his head or if there was something truly connecting them that he couldn't quite grasp, but he leaned on her as he Healed.

And because she was there...he could.

CHAPTER 6

AIMEE SWAYED but stood strong as she watched the flesh on Parker's chest knit itself together. She'd never seen anything like it, and from the way the others watched in astonishment, she wasn't sure they had either. She'd known Walker was a Healer, but *this*...this was unlike anything she could have imagined.

And now she had a glimpse of why Walker had said he *needed* to Heal her.

Because it was his gift.

But from the way his own skin grayed, and how his breathing became labored, she knew his power came with a price. So she held onto him and gave him everything she had, even if it was just on a mental level that told him she was there for him. She stood there, as strong as she could be for him.

That tug within her chest pulled again, and she willingly let some part of her escape. It wasn't like when she ached from her curse, it was something *more*. Somehow, she *knew* it was because of Walker.

What that connection—however imaginary or fragile —was, she wasn't sure, but she would find out.

As soon as Parker was Healed, or at least as much as he was going to be lying in a field right outside the den wards, someone pulled up in a truck, and they placed Parker in the back of it with Avery and Brandon each near his head. Parker was conscious at that point, doing his best to reassure his mates that everything was okay, and repeatedly saying that Walker was a damned magician.

Aimee might not be sure about the former, but she wholeheartedly agreed with the latter after watching the magic flow through Walker's skin and into Parker's. She'd watched as he put everything he had into his gifts as Healer. He hadn't stopped trying to save Parker, even when his own body looked as though it were taking a beating.

While she didn't know exactly how his magic worked, she knew just from watching him that he'd pulled energy from himself to Heal Parker. It had to hurt, even though it wasn't like in some of the stories online where they said that he took the injuries on himself. Humans were constantly wondering how shifters worked and what magic they held, and it led to a lot of false information. She'd never wanted to believe that Parker's burn marks would show up on Walker, and was honestly relieved that while Walker's skin looked far paler and clammier than it had before, it was still burn-free.

From what she'd seen, he'd already sacrificed so much of himself for his Pack, and she wasn't sure she'd be able to hold herself back from trying to stop him if he pushed more.

But he was doing well, and Parker would be okay—at least she hoped he would from what she had seen. And it wasn't as if she had any right to tell Walker what to do. She just had an odd attraction to him, same as he when it came to her. That didn't mean she could hold him back from doing what his Pack bonds needed him to do. She wouldn't stand in the way of that.

Why she even thought to try, she didn't know.

Strong hands slid over her shoulders, and she leaned into Walker as he stepped up beside her. She'd have known who he was from his presence alone, and while that might have seemed weird before knowing about magic and shifters, right then, it felt as if it were her new normal.

"We need to get you inside the den wards just in case this was only the first attack," Walker grumbled, his voice low and a little raspy. He usually almost drawled with a quiet strength, but he sounded a bit exhausted. She couldn't blame him, considering how much better Parker had looked when they drove away compared to the horror he'd been in when the fire attacked him. She'd never seen anything like it, and she was so glad that she and Walker were close enough to help him when he needed it.

As Walker's words penetrated her slow thoughts, she stiffened. It honestly hadn't occurred to her that she could be in danger. Not with the adrenaline that had been running through her system and the power of the wolves surrounding her. Walker had protected her, had literally thrown his own body over hers even though he was the Healer and there was no one there to Heal him.

And while the seriousness of the situation crept into her bones, so did her worry for the man who only thought of others, never himself.

"As long as you come with me," she said firmly.

He gave her a strange look and then pulled her closer. She wasn't even sure he was aware he'd done the latter. "Of course. I'm not leaving you alone."

She did her best not to warm at the thought. He was just being protective because that was who Walker was. Nothing more.

He held her hand once again as he led her through the wards. Since she wasn't a wolf or Pack, she had to be led in by someone who'd invited her or the wards—and then the sentries who guarded the gates—wouldn't let her in.

"Will Parker be okay?" she asked softly once they were through. She had kept that question to herself not only because she didn't know who else was around that might hear, but because she'd been afraid of the answer. What if Parker wasn't as okay as he looked? She didn't know anything about Healing or burns such as his—she barely understood what was going on with her.

Walker squeezed her hand and nodded as they made their way to a small home on the outskirts of the woods that was situated right behind the clinic. She'd never been to this particular place before, so she didn't know where she was. "He will." Walker opened the door after pressing his palm against the scanner and gestured for her to go inside. "Come on in. We can talk for a bit. This is my place, and we're right behind the clinic if they need us. Leah is taking over Parker's case for now, so I can restore my reserves since that took a lot out of me. And since she's a water witch, she'll be able to take care of him better than I could at this point anyway."

Aimee nodded and stepped into Walker's house, her gaze landing on everything at once as she tried to think about what to say. "Leah is Ryder's mate, right? He's the Heir?"

"Yeah. Until Fallon, Gideon and Brie's daughter, is

older and can handle the mantle of power that comes with that. She'll one day be the Heir, then the Alpha when the time comes. Once the next generation grows up, they slowly start to take our positions. Though I will always be a Healer, eventually, I might not be *the* Healer with as much connection to the wolves as I have now."

She wasn't sure how he felt about that considering he kept his voice in lecture-mode, but maybe one day she would ask. Not that she was sure she had that many days left, but she wasn't going to think about that right now.

"Okay, so you said that you needed to replenish your reserves. What can we do for you to make that happen?" She paused, her brain finally catching up to where they were. "Oh, and did you want me to go back to Mitchell and Dawn's? Or even my own apartment? Because if you need space, and if the Pack needs to regroup or something while they figure out what happened, I'll totally get out of your hair."

Or fur.

Oh, great, now she was making internal jokes and letting her mind wander. Being so close to Walker without anyone around was apparently making her lose part of her sanity.

Walker cupped her cheek, forcing her brain to stop going in a thousand different directions and only focus on him. "We're here because Dawn and Mitchell are on their way to the Centrals to ensure that there aren't any issues there. Most of my other family members are either on patrol, trying to see what the hell happened, or with Gideon right now, forming a plan. As I'm not a fighter and in need of food to restore my energy, I'm at home. I told them I'd bring you with me so you'd be out of danger."

And probably out of the way, as well, but neither of them said that. She wasn't sure where she stood with the others in the Pack, but right then, it didn't matter. Not yet, anyway.

"How on earth do you know all of that?"

Walker shrugged and pulled her toward the kitchen where he started taking out fixings for a sandwich. "Some texted me what was going on, and some of the other soldiers were around when we were putting Parker in the truck and explained it to me."

She pushed him gently out of the way and forced him onto one of the barstools in the kitchen. "Let me make you some food. You rest."

"I can handle it," he grumbled, ever the wolf.

"It's a sandwich. Let me help, okay? I can't do much right now since I'm not a shifter, not Pack, and I don't even have a freaking job, but I can help you eat. Just let me know what you want on it, and I'm there." She hadn't meant to blurt all of that out and sound so useless, but it wasn't as if she could really help herself. She was so far out of her depth, it wasn't funny.

"I like everything I pulled out of the fridge," Walker said patiently. He was always so damn patient...except when he had her in his arms for those few brief kisses, then, he wasn't so unflappable.

She was sure her cheeks were bright red, and Walker probably knew exactly what she was thinking about given his knowing look, but she ignored it.

Aimee quickly made him two large sandwiches before making herself a small one since she was suddenly hungry, as well. She took the seat beside him and nibbled at her food as he practically inhaled his. They talked about nothing in particular, but the sound of his voice soothed her, as did the fact that the color was slowly coming back to his skin. Apparently, food helped him replenish his stores, but she had a feeling resting would help even more. However, she didn't know his plans for the rest of the day, nor did she know what was going on with the rest of the Pack.

"Who do you think tried to hurt Parker?" she asked abruptly.

Walker tilted his head as if he were truly a wolf and studied her face. "Why do you think the attack was aimed at Parker specifically?"

"You don't?" she asked, frowning. "The fire didn't

touch a single other person and looked as if it came from four corners to center around Parker. I know you pushed me down so the fire wouldn't hit us, but it was still high enough before it hit Parker that it might not have touched as at all."

Walker shook his head. "It went low enough." He held out his arm, and Aimee sucked in a breath before gently tracing her fingers over a red mark on his skin.

"Walker, do you need to see Leah?" She jumped up from her chair and went to get ice or something to help, but Walker put his palm on her arm, stalling her.

"I'm fine, Aimee." Once again, his voice was a low rumble that went straight to parts of her she'd long forgotten.

She turned so she faced him while he sat on the stool at the kitchen counter. He was already far taller than she was, and in this position, he seemed even larger. Yet she wasn't afraid of him, and couldn't fathom a reason why she would be other than the feelings he stirred within her.

Aimee cleared her throat, pushing those thoughts out of her mind as far as she was able.

"What are you thinking about?" Walker asked, his gaze on hers.

"Parker?" It was a question more than an answer—and a lie. She should have been thinking about Parker and the rest of the Pack. She should have been thinking about what the next steps would be and how she could stay out of the way since she was an outsider in something far bigger than she.

But she wasn't thinking any of that.

Instead, she was thinking about how much she liked the feeling of Walker's skin on hers as his thumb gently brushed the inside of her forearm. And she thought about how good his hands would feel on other parts of her body.

She might not be as strong as she once was, but she was still a living, breathing woman who, apparently, had needs that had decided to show up and consume her right at that moment.

"No, you're not." Walker kept his grip on her arm even as he slid from the stool. The action brushed their bodies together, and she sucked in a breath. "I'm not either. Not beyond the fact there is nothing we can do about that particular situation for now. If and when the time comes, I'll be ready to help out where I'm needed. But for now, it's just you and me in the room, and I think we should finish what we were talking about in the field before everything happened."

She blinked, still keeping her gaze on his. "I don't think we were were doing much talking at that point." She blushed, aware she was far more brazen than usual and *liking* it.

His other hand came up, his thumb gently brushing a

soft caress over her lips. "Maybe we should talk first, though that's not exactly what I said on the field."

Disappointment slid through her, and she tried not to let it show. She must not have been successful because he lowered his head to rest his forehead on hers.

"I'm only saying that because if I start kissing you while we're both alone in my house, I'm not going to stop unless you ask me to."

"And I probably won't want you to," she said wryly, truthfully.

He let out a rough chuckle she could feel along her body. "That honesty of yours is going to get us into trouble." She could hear the smile in his voice as he said it, so she figured it wasn't all that bad. "That means I should get what I have to say out in the open now before we go too far and can't take it back."

She pulled away, her brows lowered. "Now you're starting to scare me a bit."

"I don't mean to. I can promise you that." He took in a deep breath, then met her eyes. "I think my wolf wants you as his mate, but with the mating bonds in flux as they are, I'm not fully sure. I don't know if I will be certain at all until we *try* mating. That means, I'd mark you as mine and hope that it's a true mating. Or, perhaps, the mating bond can start with us as soon as we have sex. Mating bonds aren't as clear as they used to be, and I'm still trying to figure out what it all means. But before I kiss you again, before I *want* you more than I already do, I have to explain it to you. You have to know that if we go to bed, we could end up mates. Before, when bonding was clear-cut, I could have warned you fully; now, I can only say it *could* happen."

Aimee took a step back, trying to formulate her words so she wouldn't hurt him or herself. "You know, I knew something was different between us. But, Walker? I'm not a wolf. I'm not Pack. So I need you to slow it down so I can catch up."

He ran a hand through his longer-than-normal hair and nodded. "I get that. And I'm making a muck-up of everything since it's not like I have a handbook for what to say when I think I've met my mate who happens to be human and *also* happens to, probably, have a curse on her. I swear, I'm usually smoother than this, or at least a little gentler, but I don't know what the hell I'm doing, and since I'm fucking it all up, I have a feeling I'm just pushing you away before we even have a chance to really talk about what's going on."

She reached out quickly and gripped his wrist. As he was a wolf and could have moved far faster to get out of her way, she knew he'd let her grab him.

"You're not pushing me away, but you're also going to have to remember I'm *human*. Yes, I'm attracted to you."

Once again, she blushed. "And let me tell you, I don't normally blurt that out to guys like that but, apparently, this is different between us, and a whole new situation for me."

He let out a small growl, and she widened her eyes. "Sorry, best not mention other *guys* in front of me right now. The mating urge is riding me just a bit, and it's making my wolf a little more aggressive than usual." He swallowed hard, and she watched the long lines of his throat work. "I'm not as dominant as most of my brothers. They were even growlier when they first met their mates. And while I'm not a hundred percent certain you're mine, I'm not pushing the possibility out of the way either."

"That should probably scare me—the growling thing. But considering I've watched my best friend turn into a wolf and fight to protect my friends and me *and* found out I have a curse on me that is causing me to slowly fade away? This isn't the weirdest conversation I've had recently."

Walker's lips quirked up into a smile, and she smiled back. He was truly handsome when he smiled, and even when he growled, and that was why she was able to say what she needed to say next.

"Walker," she said slowly, her voice serious now, "you know that I'm sick, that I might not have a lot of time left." She didn't let the tears fall, she'd already had time to grieve what she might lose because of the unknown. "First, I truly hope that what you're saying is because of *me* and not a way to Heal me."

She hadn't known she was worried about that until she'd said the words.

Walker's eyes suddenly glowed gold, and she let out a gasp. "That is *not* the issue. I am not feeling *pity* for you. Fuck, nothing I'm feeling for you has anything to do with *pity*."

She didn't back down, even when he started to growl low in his chest. "Fine. I believe you, but I also had to ask." She raised her chin, her breath holding steady. "I've been pitied enough in my life for how poor my family was or how, no matter how hard I tried to pay for college, I always ended up having to drop out for one circumstance or another. I've seen pity in even my friends' eyes when they realized I would probably always be a waitress at a small diner rather than anything more. I saw their pity when I couldn't even hold that job because I was sick. So I'm sorry if the first thing that came to mind was pity and not the fact that you could want me for me."

He crushed his mouth to hers then, startling her into opening her lips and letting his tongue slide in. The kiss was rough, demanding, and sent heated shivers down her spine and all the way to her fingertips.

When he pulled away, leaving them both panting, she

curled her fingers into the cotton of his shirt and tried to catch her breath.

"Pity has *nothing* to do with what I feel for you. *Nothing.* I don't know if you're my mate, not for sure, but I know there's something here. If you *are* my mate, and I'm able to Heal you because of it? Then that's a fucking perk, but it's not the reason I want you. Yes, I want to save you. Yes, it's in my blood to do so. But it's not the only fucking thing. You're in my dreams, Aimee. From the moment I first saw you. You haunt my sleep and my waking hours. You drive my wolf insane. I don't know what happens next, but I do know that if you want to, I want to take a chance and see if you could be mine." He swallowed hard. "And if I can be yours."

She was sure that there had been more romantic words spoken, especially in all the world over the eons of its existence, but right then, she couldn't think of any of them.

Walker's words were just what she needed, exactly what *they* needed.

And now, she needed to figure out what she wanted. Because if she took the wrong step, she could hurt them both.

"I want you," she whispered. "You already know that. But mating is permanent, Walker. I don't know if I'm ready for that yet. And, honestly, I don't know if you are either."

He lowered his head to hers, resting like he had before. "Then we take it one step at a time. We see if we *can* be, and then see if we *should* be."

Aimee leaned back so she could look into his eyes and cup his bearded cheek. "That...that sounds perfect."

In answer, he leaned down and took her lips once more.

And she was lost.

CHAPTER 7

AIMEE TASTED OF SWEETNESS, like *his,* and Walker knew if he weren't careful, he'd find himself addicted. Yet in that moment, he wasn't sure he cared. She clung to him, and he towered over her, deepening the kiss and pulling her closer. His wolf craved her, and the man wasn't far behind. She made a little sound in the back of her throat that pulled a growl out of him, and he couldn't help but run one hand down her back to grip her ass. He squeezed, shocking them both, but they didn't break apart.

Couldn't break apart.

If he were thinking only through his wolf, he'd devour her, lead her to the bedroom or even the couch in the living room behind them and strip them both down to nothing but skin. He wanted—no, he *needed*—to be inside her, even if he'd just told himself they would take it slower than they were at this present moment.

Aimee was his drug, his addition, his salvation.

And yet, he knew if he didn't stop right then, they'd go too far, too fast. He needed to remember that she was human and didn't have the same mating urges he had. Oh, yes, she could feel some connection and that attraction she'd spoken of, but it wasn't even close to the extent it would have been if she were a wolf. And because of that, going full-tilt right away would be careless, even if it were the fates and the moon goddess who started it all.

So, he would pull away and let her breathe, if only for a few moments longer.

When he finally wrenched himself away from her, they were both panting, their bodies shaking as they clung to one another as if they were lost, thirsty sailors on a vast ocean who had just found pure water in far too long.

"That was..." she whispered, her breaths shaky.

"Yeah. That was...yeah." He grinned at her, feeling lighter than he had in ages. He wasn't like the rest of his family, who had each gone through their own personal hells in order to survive their previous Pack leaders and turn into the adults they were today. Yes, his father and uncles had been harsh taskmasters, but he'd had it far easier than the rest of his brothers and sister and cousins. He'd only been forced to bear witness to the ruins that were their history and help find a way to pave the stones that would one day be their destiny.

As he'd said before, he was the Healer, not a soldier. He did not fight, but stood behind until it was his time to face danger head-on so he could help those who fell around him.

It wasn't an easy way to be seen by those who were so much stronger and fought so much harder, but he'd learned to live with it. He'd found a way to be the man who wanted a mate when the others didn't. And, one by one, they had found their true halves and thirds while he had once again been forced to stand by and watch.

Now, he had his potential future in his hands, yet he knew she could sift through his fingertips like sand on a windy day. Even without the curse, her life as a human was far shorter than his, so much more fragile. There were so many *ifs* when it came to Aimee and what she could be to him—and what she could be herself.

He had to find a way to break her curse.

Had to see if she was his mate.

Had to discover if he could change her and have her survive.

But the *only* way for her to be changed under the eyes of their new rules and upcoming laws was if she was his mate.

So the vicious cycle reared its ugly head once again,

and he held her in his arms and studied her face. He knew she was thinking just as hard as he was in that moment, but he wasn't sure where her thoughts lay. Maybe one day it would be his honor and *duty* to find out.

Before he could ask her what their next step should be —because while he might have wanted to just tell her outright, he'd learned from the women in his family not to be that much of an asshole—his phone buzzed in his pocket.

He gave her an apologetic smile and pulled it out so he could answer. "Sorry, I have to take this."

She waved him off. "Of course, you do. You're not only the Healer, but Parker was *just* attacked by a witch. I'll give you privacy."

He held her hand so she wouldn't leave him. If he needed to talk in private, he would, but for now, he couldn't let her out of his sight. His wolf—and the man— had it bad.

"Gideon, what can I do for you?" Walker asked, his voice harsher than usual. He wasn't angry that his brother and Alpha had interrupted, considering the fact that he'd needed time to get his thoughts in order anyway. But since his cock was currently pressing into his zipper and his wolf was riding him hard, he wasn't surprised that he sounded off.

"Come over to the house so we can talk about what's

going on with the attack. Leah said Parker's resting, and she will update us soon. I just got off the phone with her and Ryder. The others have done their reconnaissance, so we're going to discuss everything each of us knows, try to piece it together, and see what we should do next."

"Okay." He paused. "I have Aimee with me."

Gideon let out a wry laugh. "We assumed since one of Kameron's soldiers saw you walk way with her, but in the future, make sure you let Dawn know if you plan to kidnap one of her friends. It's only because she and Mitchell are at the Central den that she's not on your doorstep right now making sure her friend is safe."

Walker cleared his throat. He'd been so focused on getting not only Parker and his mates safely out of harm's way, but also Aimee, that he hadn't exactly mentioned to Dawn where he was taking her friend. Yes, he'd known where everyone else had gone, but he hadn't thought to mention himself. He was so used to not having to keep others up-to-date because he was usually at the clinic or at their side on the field.

"Next time, I'll do better. Do you want Aimee to come with me?" He met her gaze, and she raised her brow. "She's standing right next to me, by the way."

She rolled her eyes, and he couldn't help but grin. She was making him act irrationally, and he didn't know if he liked it. But he knew he didn't want it to stop either.

"I can leave," she mouthed, and he shook his head. He didn't want her to go yet, and he knew he probably wouldn't get what he wanted anyway.

"Dawn and Mitchell are on their way back to the den. Why don't you drop her off at their place since we're discussing Pack business? While I trust Aimee, she's also not Pack, and some of the other members that won't be at the meeting because of seniority might have a problem with that."

Their Pack had gone through some changes recently and had had a few upheavals. It seemed that every time they got back on their feet, something else happened to make them fight harder. While Walker understood that Aimee truly had no place at an official hierarchy meeting, he still didn't want her out of his sight. His wolf rode him hard, and he had a feeling he'd have to start fighting his other half back sooner rather than later if he wanted to remain sane and keep her from fearing him and his wolf. After all, she might know about some of the world of the paranormal, but she didn't know everything about what wolves and mating entailed.

"Understood," Walker said quickly after he'd been silent for far too long. "Be there soon." He hung up and stuffed his phone back into his pocket.

"I need to drop you back off at Dawn's and then check on Parker before heading over to Gideon's." He cleared this throat. "Once I'm done, though, I'd like to see you again. To *talk* about what just happened."

She gave him a shy smile. "Talk? Yes, we need to talk. And I think some space right now might be good for both of us. I have a feeling neither of us can think clearly when we're in each other's presence.

He kissed her again, knowing he shouldn't, and had a feeling she was far more correct in that statement than she could possibly know.

An hour later, Walker sat in Gideon's large living room as his Alpha paced the floor, Kameron, right beside him. As the Enforcer, Kameron was probably just as on edge as the Alpha since his triplet *should* have been able to sense that danger was coming. But since his brother hadn't been able to, they all knew that something was wrong.

Though because they were the Talon Pack in this new world, something was *always* wrong. Even if it only felt that way.

A wave of peace slid over him, and Walker raised a brow at Brandon. His brother was the Omega of the Pack, meaning he could help soothe the emotional strain within the Pack bonds and settle the intense anger or insecurities that sometimes filled the room so thickly that Walker could practically taste it. While Walker Healed the body, Brandon healed the soul.

Though Walker put his whole heart and energy into what he did for his patients, he knew their gifts took an even greater toll on Brandon. Now that his brother had two mates to lean on, however, he'd been able to use his gifts a lot easier. Hence why he was able to help now, even when one of those mates was back at the clinic with Leah, resting.

Walker watched as some of the tension in Kameron's shoulders released, and the Enforcer paused his pacing before glaring at Brandon. The three of them were triplets among the large family of siblings and shared a connection beyond the many others they had with the rest of the family, hierarchy, and Pack, and none of them liked when they used their gifts on each other. Kameron, in particular, shoved off any type of energy that came through the bonds that might interfere with how he wanted to feel or think.

"Cut it out, Brandon," Kameron growled.

Gideon raised a brow at the two before shaking his head. "Emotions are running high, and we'll make mistakes if we don't step back and think, Kameron. Let Brandon do his job. He's not manipulating any of us, he's just letting us focus as a group rather than ratchet up each other's anger until we go to war without going through all of our options."

Kameron glared before stalking to an empty seat on the couch. "I'm fine," he snapped, and they all knew it was a lie. There was nothing *fine* about what had happened to Parker, and nothing would be *fine* until they figured out if the magic was indeed connected to the fire witch and, therefore, Blade and the Aspen Pack.

Gideon gave Kameron a look before he went to stand in front of the fireplace.

"We all knew that Blade would do something when he found a way to hurt us without getting caught," Gideon began. "And while we don't have clear evidence it was him, the magic was that of a fire witch."

"There is more than one fire witch in the world," Brie, Gideon's mate said softly. "Our Pack has two, and the Redwoods even have one as their Enforcer. Just because the attack on the field was attempted by a fire witch, doesn't mean it was performed by the fire witch we have in mind."

"That's all true," Kameron said with a growl. "But there is only one fire witch who has already taken a member of this Pack and killed one of the Centrals. And *that* witch is Blade's. She scarred and hurt our Pack members before, and I have a feeling she won't stop anytime soon.

Max, who sat beside Kameron, stiffened, bringing the attention of the room to him. The witch may not have scarred him, but his body and soul still bore the marks from their last war. None of them wanted to be put in the middle of another one—Max, least of all.

Walker cleared his throat, and the others looked at him. He hated being the center of attention, but he also didn't want Max to be the one under scrutiny.

"What's the plan?" Walker asked. "Because while we *know* Blade is up to something, we don't know if it's the whole Pack. Their Beta, Audrey, seems to be on our side, though she's under a gag order thanks to the Alpha's edict. So what do we do? Attack the Aspens for attacking one of ours? Go covertly and take out Blade? I'm not sure what would cause the least amount of bloodshed."

Avery stood up suddenly from Brandon's side. Her eyes went glassy, and she blinked a few times before Brandon stood up and brought her to his chest. The fact that she was here with them and not sitting by Parker's side told Walker that their foreseer had known she needed to be in this meeting and this was the reason why.

"This won't be the end," she said quietly, her voice hollow. "He's waiting. He didn't get what he wanted. So he will strike again. This time, closer to home."

She fell back against her mate's chest, and Walker immediately went to them both so he could check her vitals. Sometimes, seeing parts of the future took its toll on her body even more than it did her mind and soul. Thankfully, she only looked tired and confused and nothing worse. There were no nosebleeds or broken capillaries in her eyes. This vision must have only been a small one compared to others she'd had in the past.

"That wasn't too helpful," Avery said, her voice scratchy.

Walker moved out of the way as Brie slid between them with a glass of water held out for Avery. Brie was the Alpha female and a submissive wolf, and she was always first in line when it came to caring for others.

"It's better than nothing," Walker said softly, meeting Brandon's gaze. His triplet nodded before moving to the side, Avery in his arms.

"I'm taking her to the clinic," Brandon said at once.

Avery waved him off though she didn't move to get down from his arms. "I'm fine. I don't need the clinic. Walker's right here."

"I know he's right here, and I know you're fine. But we're going to let you lie down next to Parker where I can watch both of you heal up." Brandon wasn't usually the forceful one of the triad, or even amongst the Brentwoods in their entirety, but when it came to protecting his mates, he tended to act more dominant.

Walker stood by and watched them walk away, a seed

of jealousy in his gut. He wanted that, *had* wanted something like that for years, but he hadn't been able to find his mate even though he was looking. He'd been in search of the one person to complete his soul since before the mating bonds changed a couple of years ago, and now it seemed like he might have his chance.

To say he was overwhelmed was an understatement.

Gideon ran a hand over his face as Brandon and Avery left before looking back at the rest of the occupants of the room.

"It's got to be Blade," his Alpha said with a sigh. "But I don't know what we're going to do about it. Yet."

"We can't go to war," Ryder said quietly. "Not again. Not so soon after the Unveiling."

"The Aspens are stronger than we are," Kameron growled. "That's a fact."

"Because they haven't had two wars in as many decades," Walker put in. "They've been in hiding without demons or demented Alphas—beyond the one they have now. They've *had* to remain hidden to keep their cats and whatever the heck else they have behind their wards secret. Because, come on, there might just be something more out there at this point. But in doing that, they've been able to grow stronger."

Parker had helped them all rank each and every Pack that he'd been able to visit, and while the Talons and

Redwoods were the most visible at the moment, the Aspens had the most power. If the Talons and their allies went up against them right then, they'd lose, and everyone in this room knew it. And even if they somehow found a way to survive an all-out battle, they'd be out to the public and susceptible to whatever punishment the humans had for them for breaking the tender truce they had salvaged.

Walker wasn't sure what would happen next, but he knew their steps needed to be confident and careful or they could lose everything they'd fought so hard to keep over the past few years.

"We're going to figure this out," Gideon said slowly, a promise in his words. "We're not going to act rashly and get our innocents killed because we want revenge. That's not who we are, and I'll be damned if we become our fathers."

Walker nodded and listened as they planned their reconnaissance and decided what the next steps would be. He wouldn't be joining them on these trips, however. His place was back in the den, keeping his people healthy and safe. It should probably bother him more that he wasn't on the front lines, but that wasn't who he was, wasn't who his wolf was.

He wasn't a soldier, he was a Healer.

Always.

CHAPTER 8

THE NEXT DAY, Aimee wasn't sure where she stood, but she was thankful she at least still had her small apartment to sit in and formulate a plan. A strategy that consisted of figuring out what to do with her life and future, but it was something.

After Dawn and Mitchell had shown up the previous day at her home, she'd tried to figure out what exactly had happened and soon realized that since she wasn't Pack, there wasn't a lot they could tell her. And while she understood, she'd also felt in the way. So, since she'd been feeling better after her passing-out incident at her now-former job, she'd eventually decided to leave the house and head back to her apartment so she could sleep in her own bed.

Walker hadn't contacted her in the interim, however,

and she wasn't sure how she should take that. He had her number since he'd gotten *all* the girls' numbers after the attack outside Dawn's former café when they all found out that Dawn was a shifter, but he hadn't used it. Not once.

And because that made her sound like a petulant teenager instead of a woman who had far bigger things on her plate than whether a boy would call her or not, she shoved that thought aside and went about updating her resume.

She might not have the higher education needed for many jobs, and frankly, she wasn't sure she had enough time left on this plane of existence to make use of her resume or the skills she did have—a thought that sent shivers through her system—but she wasn't about to stand by and let the world pass her by while she sat around feeling sorry for herself.

So she would find a job so she could pay for groceries and her tiny apartment, and perhaps once again set some aside to help her family who was constantly in even direr straits than she was. And while she did all of that, she'd find a way to cure whatever the hell was wrong with her because she wasn't about to give up without a fight. And in so doing, if she ended up near Walker more often than not...then it would set her up to do the other thing on her list.

Live in the moment.

Living in the moment right then meant holding a man close that made her feel something more than just casual pity and being invisible. He listened to her as she spoke and clearly wanted her from how their conversations had gone.

If she was his mate? Well then, that was something they'd both have to deal with. Because while she wanted him with every breath she took, she was truly afraid what would happen to him if he couldn't break her curse and ended up losing her not as a friend, but as a *mate*.

While she didn't know all the details of Mitchell and Dawn's mating, she knew enough to understand that Mitchell had lost a mate years ago and that it had broken him to the point where he'd almost lost out on Dawn.

Could she do that to Walker?

Before she could bury herself farther down into her never-ending cycle of thoughts, there was a light knock on her door. She frowned.

Who on earth could that be?

But as soon as she neared the door, she knew. There was only one person in the world that made her body ache and the hairs on her arms stand on end in anticipation just from his mere presence. And the fact that he could do that through the solid wood of the door just reminded her of how potent he truly was.

Quiet Walker Brentwood with that casual drawl and soft smile made her burn like no other.

Knowing she was stalling, she quickly opened the door so he stood right in front of her—this towering wolf who said he wasn't as dominant as others. She didn't know what he was talking about because the man dominated the room and he wasn't even standing in it yet.

"Walker," she said, then cleared her throat because she sounded far too breathy.

His gaze traveled over her body and ended on her face with a look of stark hunger that she had a feeling mirrored her own. There was something about Walker that pulled her toward him, and if she weren't careful, she knew she could fully lose herself with him without bothering to wonder who she had been before she met him.

"You weren't at Dawn and Mitchell's when I got out of the meeting, so I figured you needed some time to breathe and perhaps think about everything that happened. I should have called before I came over, but I wanted to see you."

She swallowed hard, ignoring the way her heart beat rapidly at his words. Walker, however, narrowed his eyes at her pulse, and she had a feeling he knew what he did to her, shifter senses and all that.

"I figured they not only needed some time alone since they're newly mated, but they also needed time to talk about Pack things that would be easier done without a human around to make things more complicated."

She stepped back and let him in because she was only now aware that she'd left him on her tiny porch where anyone could probably hear her talking about Packs and humans. Her walls were not only thin, but her neighbors also constantly left their doors open for ventilation. It wasn't the safest way to live, but it wasn't as if she were one of the ones doing that. She closed the door behind her and tried to suck in air, but being near Walker didn't make that easy.

"That makes sense," Walker said. "By the way, your neighbors aren't home if that's what you're worried about. I assume they're all at work or school, given the hour of the day."

"Oh, yeah, that makes sense. Sorry, I try not to blurt out that I know what I do about the Packs in case random people find out who don't need to know." She could feel her cheeks heat at her words. "I guess I watch too many spy movies or something."

Walker reached out and cupped her face, the action settling her as it heated her body. "Considering what Dawn and some of the others have gone through over the past few years, I think you being cautious is a good thing." He frowned as he looked over her small apartment, and it got her back up, though she knew she shouldn't be ashamed of what she could afford. "I don't know if I feel comfortable with you being out like this with so little protection."

"I've been just fine on my own for a long time." Too long, considering her age, but she didn't need to tell him about her family's issues. "This is what I have, and nothing truly awful has happened to me. Except for the curse. Have any leads on that yet?" She had no idea who had possessed her body right then and made her sound like Cheyenne or Dhani, but she could have rightly put her hand over her mouth in shock.

Walker didn't look annoyed, though; instead, he let out a sigh and seemed to take the words to heart. "I don't have any yet, but I'm researching and talking to our local Coven."

Aimee quickly went to him and put her hand on his arm. "I didn't mean to take my own issues with my apartment out on you. I *know* you're working on what's wrong with me even with all the other things you have to deal with. Don't think I'm unaware of that fact, and I truly appreciate it. I'm sorry I got a little short."

His brows rose, and he pulled his arm away so he could tangle their fingers together. She shouldn't have let her heart beat faster once again at the touch, but she couldn't help it.

"I'm lost," Walker said. "Explain to me. Slowly."

She winced but didn't let go of his hand. "I thought when you looked around my place you were finding it lacking, and I got my back up. I'm not usually one to get snippy like that since I generally leave it to my friends who have better comebacks."

He shook his head before reaching out to cup her face. "That's not why I looked around your place. I like it. It suits you, and I like the way you decorated. I was only glowering like I did because, as a wolf, I'm always looking for holes in defense and protection. My brother Kameron is worse because of his job. My wolf wants to make sure you're safe and practically wrapped in bubble wrap. The man knows that's not how things work in the human world—not even in the shifter world to be honest—and finding that balance is difficult when all I want to do is strip you down and mark you as mine."

His eyes had gone gold as he spoke, yet she felt no fear, only eagerness.

"Oh," she said softly, not sure she could formulate any other words at that point.

"Oh," he repeated. "*Oh* just about covers it, don't you think?" He let out a ragged breath but, thankfully, didn't pull away. "I came here to talk to you, to get to know you so my wolf would be somewhat satisfied, and you and I could go through things slowly, but I don't think I know how to do that."

Aimee knew there were smart things to say just then. Things like how they should talk about Parker, her curse, the ramifications of mating and what it would mean if she were brought into the Pack with or without a mating bond. All of those things had been brought up recently in front of her, and they were constantly playing in a loop in the back of her mind.

Yet all she could do was lean forward and kiss the bottom of his scruffy chin.

Today, she could be the Aimee she'd wanted to be for so long, the woman who *felt* and lived in the now. Soon, she could and *would* deal with the consequences of her actions and decide what would be the next course for her life—as well as Walker's. But for now, she would do what she'd wanted to do before, what she'd *needed* to do, and just *be*.

"We can get to know each other and talk about all the important things. After."

His eyes, if possible, went even brighter. "After." Not a question, a growl.

"After."

Then he was on her, his lips demanding, his hands searching, and Aimee knew she was lost and had no desire to find her way out of this passion until perhaps it was too late.

His hands slid through her hair, the pencil she'd used

to hold her loose bun in place dropping to the linoleum tile, the sound of its echo blunt and unadorned in the silence of her apartment.

She trailed her hands up the soft cotton of his button-down shirt before gripping the fabric in her fists. She was only human and had nowhere near the strength he did, but she had a feeling if she tugged hard enough, she'd tear his shirt right off. Lust did that to a woman—human or no.

"I want you," he growled against her lips, and the tenor of it went straight to her core.

"Then have me, but I need you, too."

"I'll be as gentle as I can, Aimee. You deserve that. You deserve soft. You deserve so much more than what I can give you right now."

She went to her toes and bit his lip. "I don't want gentle. I want *you*. And even as hard and rough as you can be, I know you won't hurt me." She didn't know how she knew that to the depths of her soul, but she did. "It's just you and me tonight. Tomorrow, the world can come at us, and we'll deal. Tomorrow, we can process the forevers and bonds and everything that could be."

She didn't know where the words had come from, only that they'd needed to be said.

"Tomorrow," he promised. "Tomorrow, we will talk about what it means to be a mate and what it means to be *mine* in truth. Tomorrow, we can discuss serious things. Today, we can just *be*."

He kissed her again, this time lifting her up by cupping her butt. She wrapped her legs around his waist and sucked in a breath as the action brought his rock-hard erection against her heat. She kept her mouth on his, even as she rocked in his hold, getting closer and closer to coming just from touching alone.

Walker had no issues finding her bedroom as it was the only door other than the bathroom in her apartment. Before she could protest, he had her on her back on the bed and hovered over her, his eyes glowing and his mouth parted.

She'd never seen anything sexier.

"This first round might go a little fast," he said with a slight laugh. "I'm not as young as I once was."

He was over a hundred but looked and *felt* as if he were in the prime of his life. Shifter genes were good for many things, and endurance, at least according to Dawn, was one of them.

"That's not what I hear," Aimee teased. "But fast for the first time,"—meaning there would be more than one time—"works for me."

He fell on her then, his wolf in his voice and eyes as he stripped her down. Thankfully, he let her strip him as well, and soon, they were both bare under her soft bedroom lights with nothing but their heavy breathing filling the space.

He looked like a rugged cowboy. She didn't know why, as she'd never seen him wear a hat and he was completely naked with his corded muscles, wide shoulders, and narrow waist. But in her head, that slight drawl went to cowboy, and that turned her on.

Of course, while his body was perfection in every way —even the slight scars that touched his skin showcased his strength—she couldn't keep her eyes off his cock. It was long, thick, and so hard, she was afraid that he'd truly fill her with one thrust.

And she couldn't wait.

"You're so beautiful," he whispered, his hands slowly sliding down her ribcage to her hips. Her gaze lifted from his groin to his face, her body blushing at how long she must have had her eyes on that particular part of his anatomy.

"I've lost too much weight," she said, aware that he could see her ribs if she sucked in deep breaths. She couldn't keep the weight on, not anymore, and they both knew the reason why. When he pressed his finger to her lips, she knew they wouldn't be talking about it anymore for the moment.

"Shifters cannot carry or share diseases, nor can they get anyone pregnant unless they are mated. And since that is not something we are completing tonight even if we can, we don't need to use condoms unless you want to. But if that's the case, I need to go get one."

She shook her head. "I trust you." That, and she'd read up on shifters as well as listened to Dawn's stories.

He lowered himself over her and kissed her, his hands roaming over her breasts. She gripped his upper arms, then his back as he plucked and pinched at her nipples, each careful touch and stroke bringing her closer and closer to completion. And when he slid his hand between her legs and touched her, she shook. He only had to brush his calloused fingers along her clit, and she broke for him, arching against his body, her legs falling to the sides as she came.

"Open your eyes," he growled against her lips, and she did as he asked. Though he hadn't actually been asking, had he?

Then he was inside her, filling her to the point of pain, yet it was such an exquisite agony that she knew she'd have him seared on her soul until the end of her days— however long that was.

"Walker," she gasped, arching against him.

"You're so fucking tight, Aimee," he growled in her ear. "I'm lost."

She wasn't sure she was supposed to hear that last part, and it only urged her on. They moved as one, their bodies arching and sliding against one another until soon, she was coming again, and he was shouting her name.

She knew she could get lost in this man, this wolf, this Healer, and never care that she'd be a different person in his arms. With one mark that might come later when they knew each other's souls more than a bare whisper of touch, he could be hers forever just as she could be his.

Only, it couldn't last forever. How could it when the world shattered around her?

Walker pulled slowly out of her before lying next to her and holding her close. His heartbeat under her ear matched her own rapid pace, and she realized she could sleep right then, though she knew they both wanted more.

Aimee sat up straight, her body jerking left, then right, then arching until she swore her spine would break. In the distance, she could hear Walker's shouts as he tried to calm her screams, but that didn't make any sense. He was right next to her, had been naked and sweaty, wrapped around her equally naked and sweaty body. Yet he sounded so far away, as if he couldn't catch her when she fell—not that he wouldn't try.

Her body convulsed, and her jaw tightened; her stomach rolled, and her muscles felt as though they were being stripped from her bones.

Then, as quickly as the pain had come, it dissipated, leaving her system in a shocking vacuum instead of the gentle ebb that it had been in since before the attack at the diner.

"Aimee, talk to me. What can I do?" Walker's gaze and hands slid over her body as he checked her for injuries, but she knew he wouldn't find any—none that he could see anyway.

She blinked at him, then let out a slow moan as he touched the skin above her upper lip, the glistening red on his finger a stark contrast to the pale callus on his thumb. And when she met his eyes again, she knew the truth.

They might well be mates, but it wouldn't matter in the end. She couldn't hide from her truth and problems. She could live in the now, but she needed to remember that *now* wouldn't last long.

Not nearly long enough.

CHAPTER 9

WALKER WOULD NOT FAIL.

Walker would not fail.

Walker would not fail.

And if he kept repeating that, it would be a vow, not a mere whisper beneath his breath. It was a promise, an oath etched in stone. Because there was no way he was going to allow whoever had their spindly hold on Aimee to prevail. He'd fight until the last breath left his lungs before he allowed that to happen.

And that was just one more reason why he *knew* she was his mate. It wasn't just a feeling anymore, or even a hope. He *knew*.

All wolves had potential mates out in the world, but not everyone could find them. Sometimes, it took decades to find even one, and then decades more to find another if the couple or triad chose not to mate. He only knew of a couple of instances where the human halves didn't choose each other even though their wolves did, and those potentials walked away from each other. Most of the time, it was because of wolves in love with humans who weren't their mates, or because the wolf found out that their mate was a human and already married to another.

The moon goddess might bless another with the idea that two souls could connect, but sometimes, the real world got in the way of fate.

Walker let out a breath and gripped the edge of Aimee's kitchen counter. There were no other commitments or bindings standing in his way now—only a fate left unknown and precarious due to a curse that no one even knew how to name. When she'd convulsed the night before, reminding him how precious their time was unless he figured out a way to save her, he'd feared he might lose everything before he even had a chance to fully realize it was there.

"You're growling, what's wrong?" Aimee said as she walked into the kitchen and wrapped her arms around his middle. He'd been afraid that, after everything that happened the night before, she'd shy away from him, but he shouldn't have worried. She'd told him she was all-in, even if they were living in the now as she'd put it—and that meant he would do the same.

It wasn't like he really wanted to do anything else anyway.

He turned in her hold and wrapped his arms around her, needing her close. They hadn't completed the mating bond, though his wolf had urged him to the night before. His gums had ached with the need to let his fangs out and mark her, but even then, he'd held himself in check. His wolf had held back, as well, even through the urging, because it had understood that she needed care and time.

"I'm thinking about what happened yesterday," he said, not wanting to lie to her. He wasn't the type to shield others from the truth even though he was a Healer. Or perhaps it was *because* he was a Healer that he was the way he was.

Her skin went pale, but she didn't pull way. His mate was stronger than she looked, and for that, he was grateful —though not surprised. No one could have survived what she'd gone through and not gain strength.

"Given the look on your face, I'm hoping you're talking about what we started with rather than what happened afterward."

He cupped her face and lowered his head to gently take her lips in a kiss. He couldn't stop touching her, though he knew he should because her nearness made it hard for him to think.

"Being with you...well, I'd say it completes me, but that's not only a cliché, it's not entirely accurate."

Laughter danced in her eyes, and he was glad he'd been the one to put it there. The dark circles underneath them, however, only made his wolf want to rip something apart—particularly the jugular of the witch who had done this to her.

"Being with you," he said again, "is *right*. It doesn't necessarily complete me because we are each whole people who have our own baggage and our own souls. Yet, together, I think...I think we can be stronger. We aren't two half-empty shells, but two people who could...I don't know, be better together than apart?" He was the one who blushed this time. "Sorry, I'm not good with words. I leave that to my brothers and cousins."

Max had always been good with words, actually. Though, he wasn't the same man now as he had been before the attack. If anyone was good with words now, it was probably Ryder or Kameron, the latter surprising more people than not.

She reached up and ran her hand over his scruffy cheek. He should have shaved before he came over the afternoon before, but he hadn't wanted to stay away any longer than necessary. He'd spent the morning clearing Parker so his brother-in-law could go home, and helping a pup. The little rascal had ended up high in a tree and hadn't been able to get down without scraping himself up along the bark. He'd thought he was a cat instead of a wolf, apparently. As soon as Walker was able to leave, however, he'd come to Aimee. He hadn't been able to stay away. And now that he'd had a taste of her, truly knew that she was his mate, he couldn't walk away.

Ever.

"You're not that bad," she said with a soft smile. "If anything, you're better than me. I'm the rambler, remember?"

"I like that you ramble."

She snorted, and he bent down to kiss the tip of her nose. He knew they had far more important things to deal with that day and would soon be leaving for the den, but he couldn't help but savor this little bit of normalcy in a time where nothing was close to being normal.

"I guess we need to go?" she asked, her voice soft.

He nodded but didn't pull away from her. Once they left her apartment, they'd be tossed back into their true realities. There would be no hiding from a possible war with the Aspens. The Talons and Redwoods were at a loss for what to do next. And he couldn't escape the fact that he didn't know what the next step with Aimee would be.

Would she agree to be his mate? To complete the mating bond and take a chance on forever—however long that may be—with him? When that happened, could he change her, make her Pack, and hopefully find a way for her to survive? There was so much riding on the unknown that it would cause anyone to doubt what they were thinking and the choices they were about to make.

But what Walker *did* know, was that he'd wanted a mate, and fate had provided for him, had *shown* him the brilliance and beauty that was Aimee. And if he were a lucky man—not that he'd ever truly felt like one—she would choose him, as well.

Everything else could follow that.

They took his car to the den, leaving hers at her apartment. Though she should be safe since she wasn't a Pack member. Whoever had attacked Parker seemingly had only been going for him, but Walker wasn't sure he wanted to take any chances. She smelled of him now, and any wolf or other shifter would be able to tell that she was his...yet not claimed.

And though he wasn't as visible to the public as some of the others in his den, there were some online sites that had his photo and made sure that others knew he was a shifter. Those humans who still had it out for anything *other* might hold their insecurities and prejudices against Aimee for being near him. While it might be illegal to harm someone for being a wolf or being *with* a wolf, that wouldn't stop the unhinged.

He held back his growl at that and kept his eyes on the

road, even as he spoke to Aimee about her prior job and what she was thinking of doing next. He wanted to know everything about her and was afraid he wouldn't have a lot of time to learn it all before circumstances out of their control led them to make a choice they weren't ready for.

They pulled into the den and drove through the wards that he knew hurt Aimee every time she went through them. He remembered the first time he'd watched her move through the wards and how she'd fallen into his arms. It had to be because of the curse and the way it reacted to any type of magic. Dhani had also responded oddly, he remembered, and he had a feeling he'd have to keep an eye on her, as well.

At his side, Aimee let out a shuddering breath then gave him a bracing smile. "I'm okay," she said before wrinkling her nose. "I'm not lying. I'm okay. Really. It just doesn't feel...pleasant when I go through the wards."

Walker nodded as he pulled into a space outside his clinic. "It's not getting worse, at least. The severity of it isn't intensifying each time you enter the wards."

"Well, at least there's that." She blew out a breath. "And if I were Pack, it might not happen at all, right?"

He tried not to be too hopeful that she'd been the one to bring it up. It wasn't as if the two of them hadn't talked about it. It was one of the reasons they were at the den, after all, but he still had to wonder.

"I don't think it would be as severe," he said carefully.

"But it's still a curse, and we don't know if me being mated to you and Pack or even if I were a wolf and Pack would change anything," she said quickly. "And, once again, I'm having a weird conversation that's not really a conversation. I'm hurting my brain."

She pivoted to him in her seat as he turned off the engine. "Walker?"

He turned as well and tilted his head at her tone. "Yeah?"

"I want you to know that everything we're not saying is going on two paths for me right now. One, everything I just said about the curse and what it could mean is on one path. But the other? That's what you and I mean to each other. I don't want to blend the two, as I think if we do, we'll end up thinking we only mated or tried to make *this* work because of what's wrong with me. And I don't want that to happen. I want you to know that I *do* feel a connection to you, and I wouldn't have slept with you if I didn't." She licked her lips, and he tried not to let his wolf show in his eyes at her words or that sweet-as-sin action. "That's why I'm so confused. I want to fix what's wrong, but I also want to see who and what we are to each other. But I'm afraid those two are so intertwined that you'll think that I only want you for what you can do, not for who you are."

She said the last part so quickly that he knew she was

nervous. So he did the only thing he could do, he kissed her.

When he pulled away, he knew his wolf was in his eyes, but it was the man who spoke. "We're on the same page. What we're dealing with is two parts of a whole surrounded by a thousand other pieces. I know we'll confuse the two sometimes, but I'm on the same page as you. I want to know *you* for *you*, not what the Pack or I could possibly do for you. I think...I think the curse could move our timetable up, but it might not change the end result. At least, I hope not."

She smiled then, and he knew they understood each other. "I guess we should get out since Dawn and Mitchell are standing outside the car staring at us."

He grinned, though he knew it didn't fully reach his eyes. How could it when he was still so afraid he'd fail? He'd sensed the other couple, of course, but he'd ignored them since he and Aimee had needed to get those words out.

"Let's go, then."

She let out a breath. "Let's."

"So..." Kameron drawled.

"So..." Walker repeated, doing his best to ignore his triplet.

"You brought her to a family meeting, and you both smell so much of each other it's as if you made one new scent. Does that mean you're joining the ranks of everyone else and allowing her to make an honest wolf out of you?"

Walker turned to Kameron, a frown on his face. "That's not your business right now."

His brother just shrugged. "You're my blood and, apparently, we're reincarnations of the same line, as well. I think that makes most things my business." The three triplets were the literal reincarnations of the original wolves when the moon goddess had come down to the mortal realm and had made the first wolf from a hunter. Only Brandon had truly been able to use that connection to help adjust the wards in a time of need. For now, it hadn't really shown itself to Walker and he figured it was the same for Kameron.

Walker just sighed and turned back to where he could keep an eye on Aimee and the others. Today was only a meal with the family and not all of them. The children were with their daycare staff, and his sister Brynn hadn't come as she was a Redwood now and couldn't make it to as many meals as she used to. Max hadn't attended either, but that was a whole other matter.

Walker had brought Aimee because he didn't want her out of his sight but he also wanted to show her what she could have if she took a chance on him. He *knew* he was moving far too fast when it came to her, but he couldn't help himself. He'd found the one he wanted to be with, and he didn't want to wait any longer. Once again, he wasn't like his siblings, and he honestly didn't care. Their lives had worked out, but they'd gone through hell for their matings. Walker wanted to be the one, the Talon that, just *once,* found his or her happiness without the heartache in between.

But as he watched the darkness under Aimee's eyes grow, he knew he wouldn't get that chance given how hard and long they'd have to push to be together.

"How are things going on the fire front?" Walker asked softly, though he knew every shifter in the room could hear him. It was hard to have a private conversation with wolves around.

"We're trying to get in contact with Audrey and plan a meet-up, but it's been difficult since she's had to hide her connection to us. We're also tracking down a few fire witches in the Coven to see if they know the spell behind it so we can find who cast it to begin with. Gina, the Enforcer for the Redwoods, is the only fire witch we know well, but she wasn't trained until later. And not by a fire witch. Plus, since she's half wolf, her powers have always been wonky."

Walker nodded, remembering when the woman had

mated a Talon wolf and had come into her powers. None of the Talons had been able to find mates due to the horrors and atrocities his father and uncles had committed. The moon goddess had stripped them of the ability to form mating bonds at all, and it wasn't until Gina and Quinn mated that anyone was able to find their potentials.

Now, the mating bonds were screwed up again, but Walker at least knew whom his mate was, even if it had taken longer than it should have for him to figure it out.

"If there's anything I can do, let me know. I'm talking to the Coven about Aimee, as well, but it's hard when I don't want to give them too much information." The Coven hadn't always been trustworthy, but they were making strides under their new leadership, as the existence of witches had also been revealed during the Unveiling.

Kameron let out a sigh. "Whoever cursed her deserves to rot in Hell. She seems like a nice woman with shitty luck and circumstances. Whatever happens, though, I hope she makes you happy. You, of all of us, deserve happiness."

Stunned by his brother's out-of-character words, he froze for a moment before turning to look at him, only to find that Kameron had already moved on to another part of the room, probably to say something random and startling to whoever he spoke to next. Typical Kameron.

Aimee came up to his side then, and he wrapped an arm around her shoulders. Wolves were typically more affectionate in public than humans, and though they hadn't yet created a mating bond, his wolf had already decided she was his. It would only take the humans to catch up.

"Doing okay?" Walker asked.

She shrugged, and his wolf perked up. "Just a little tired."

"We can go back to my place if you want. Let you take a nap."

"I shouldn't need a nap. I should be able to get through a simple meal without having to sit down because of sheer exhaustion."

He let out a small growl before taking her hand and leading her toward the door. "You're going to take a nap, and I'm going to do some more research. We're going to figure this out."

She tugged her arm away and frowned. "I'm fine."

"You're not."

He was aware that they had an audience, but he didn't care. Aimee was hurting, and there was nothing he could do except make sure she sat down and relaxed. His wolf was already riding him hard, and his Healing tendencies weren't helping in this situation either.

Before he could give them privacy, however, Avery

stood in front of them, her two mates behind her. Parker's skin was pink in some places, but other than that, he didn't look like he'd almost died. The fact that Parker had been closer to death's door than most knew wasn't something they were letting people know—not unless they had to. Brandon frowned at him but didn't say anything. The hairs on Walker's arm rose, and he knew something was coming...something he knew would change everything.

The room quieted as Avery met his gaze then Aimee's, his sister-in-law's eyes clouded with a vision.

"You have to make a choice and make it soon. If you wait until the darkness ebbs, it will be too late. She must be Pack, or everything will be lost. She must be *yours,* or everything will be lost."

As soon as Avery had said the final word, she passed out in her mates' arms, and Walker turned to Aimee.

They were running out of time, and now they all knew it. But what else could they do but fall into fate? He wanted Aimee to be his, but never like this, never without a true choice on her part. He just prayed that if she did say yes, if she did become his mate, it wasn't only because of what could happen if she didn't become Pack.

He wanted her to want him for who he was, but in the end, as long as she could breathe into the next day and live, he would take her however he could get her.

Love and true mating or not.

CHAPTER 10

THE ROOM EXPLODED into voices and chaos at the end of Avery's speech, and Aimee could only stand there and listen.

In the back of her mind, she could hear the words being said, but all the while, she knew she had to formulate her own thoughts and make her own choices. If she didn't, she *knew* she'd lose herself, and Walker would lose the part of him that made him the man she knew, the one she thought one day she could love.

Someone asked if Avery was okay, and she heard an answer, but Aimee didn't see who it was.

Another came to Aimee's side and held her arm, but she only focused on Walker.

"If she's mated in, she'll be Pack, Walker," Gideon said near them. "I can't make her Pack unless she's your mate or a wolf. And we can't change her unless she's already Pack thanks to the humans. And since humans— especially cursed humans—don't react well to Pack magic without a mating bond, there's only one choice if that's what you two decide to do. She'll be a Talon, Walker." She felt, more than saw Gideon turn to her. "You'll be a Talon, Aimee."

She nodded, but she only had eyes for Walker. "I...I think Walker and I need time to think."

"Not too much time," Avery said softly from Parker's arms.

Aimee was tired of curses and visions and everything out of her control. For one moment, she just wanted to feel normal. Yet she knew this *was* their normal. And the fact that all of them were willing to do what they had to in order to cure her was something she would be grateful for —once the shock of what Avery had said passed.

"Give us some air," Walker said before pulling her toward the door. They were out on the path and walking toward his house behind the clinic without saying another word, and for that, she was grateful. Even before this, everything had been moving far too fast for her, and now it was as if it were going full speed ahead with no return or stops.

Soon, she found herself standing in front of Walker in his living room with a glass of whiskey in her hand and another in his. He had poured two fingers into each, and now they toasted one another before tossing them back. It burned down her throat, and she once again wondered how the hell this had become her life.

"Okay, then," she said as he took the tumbler from her hand and set it down next to his on the coffee table.

"I honestly wasn't expecting that," Walker said slowly. "I thought we would have more time, and Avery doesn't usually have so many visions. But her mating bond with Parker and Brandon seems to have shoved them into high gear, and she's still trying to figure them out."

Aimee ran her hand through her hair before looking back up at him. "While I feel almost as if our choices are being taken away, I *know* that's not the case."

He gave her a sharp look but, thankfully, didn't say anything so she could continue.

"Since the first moment we saw each other, we knew there was a connection. And be it supernatural or just a gut feeling, we've *known*." She sucked in a deep breath, knowing she was jumping off a ledge where there would be no return. She wouldn't be the same person once she made that leap. Though, honestly, she didn't know if she was the same person she had been two days ago.

That was the thing about making decisions and coming to a crossroads in one's life. Each turn, each corner rounded, led to a new version of the person you used to be, and it was what you did with that new reality that determined which turn you'd take next.

Walker's eyes went gold, and his jaw clenched. "What are you saying, Aimee? I need you to be clear because if we take this next step, there's no going back. There's no breaking a bond if we find out the human parts of our souls aren't who we thought they were. There's no living apart from one another while we try to find ourselves because we will *always* be able to feel one another deep down in the depths of our souls. Mating isn't a way to save your life or to listen to the visions of a foreseer. Mating is forever. It's a blending of two wholes into a new existence. We'll be *mates*. Not married, not seeing if we like each other. We'll be entwined until the end of our days. And while my wolf—and the man, for that matter—would like nothing more than to take that step with you and find out who we are together as well as who we can be apart while still connected, I don't want to force any of this. I've had my whole life to think about what the moon goddess's decision would mean to me, and how I could form a personal connection with the idea that whoever my mate was, they would be perfect for me even if I didn't know them as well as I should. You've only had a few months to even understand what a mate is, what they could be, and far less time to realize that I could be that person."

Aimee stared up at him, wondering how she could

want this man so much in such a short time. Everything was slowly tumbling out of her control, and she knew if she took this step, there would be no going back.

And the strange thing was...she didn't want to.

"I don't want to think about Avery or anything that could come of this. I just want to think of you and me." She licked her lips and loved the way that, even now, his attention honed in on the action. "I want you, Walker. I want to take a chance. I know that part of this *is* because of what might happen, but only the part that is making us second-guess. I wouldn't have been with you last night if I didn't think there was a reason for us to be together beyond visions and curses. I've never taken a chance with *anything*, Walker. I've been the calm and reasonable one of my friends, the woman who never strayed out of my lane."

"And now you want to go wild?" he asked, his wolf in his eyes.

"Only with you," she said honestly. "Always, only with you."

She put her hand on his chest, her fingers tangling in his shirt. She wasn't shaking, wasn't nervous. She was *sure*. And when he looked into her eyes, she hoped he saw that.

"You'll be mine forever," he whispered, lowering his head to hers.

"As long as you're mine, too," she said back, equally as soft. "That means we'll have a long time to get to know each other."

"Trust in fate?" he asked.

"This time. This time, I can trust."

And when he kissed her, she arched into him, needing him closer than she thought possible. He slid his hand through her hair and used the other to wrap around her back and bring her closer. When he pulled away suddenly, however, she let out a sound of protest.

"I forgot to tell you exactly what happens next," he said, his breath coming in pants. "You're not a wolf, so you didn't grow up hearing what the technical parts of mating are."

She raised a brow, and he laughed.

"Not *those* parts. Well, okay, those parts too once I became a teenager. But mating happens in two stages. One is the human half, and that comes from me coming inside you."

She frowned. "Didn't you already do that?" And, yes, she knew her cheeks were pink, but if she could have sex, then she could talk about it. Somewhat.

He nodded. "Yes, but like Dawn mentioned to you, mating bonds have been difficult recently. Because we didn't go to bed knowing we wanted to create a bond, *and* we didn't complete the second part of the process, it didn't take."

Aimee swallowed hard. "And if it doesn't take this time?"

His eyes glowed gold, and he kissed her hard before answering. "It will. And when I mark you as mine, we'll connect my wolf. I would say connect my wolf to yours, but you aren't a wolf."

Yet.

That was left unsaid, and for some reason, while the idea of attaching herself to Walker for eternity didn't scare her, the idea of becoming a wolf scared the crap out of her.

"Breathe," he whispered, holding her close. "Like Gideon said, you'll be Pack and connected to me on a Healer level and through our mating bond. You won't need to be a wolf for me to try and sense those threads."

"But I'll have to change eventually," she whispered.

He leaned back to meet her eyes, the pain in his gaze so intense that she wanted to soothe him rather than letting him do it for her. So she reached out and cupped his jaw, loving the way he turned his face into her hand and kissed her palm.

"If you want to live longer than a mortal lifespan, yes." He cleared his throat. "One thing at a time, though. Okay?"

She nodded. "Mating first. Then whatever vision Avery saw. Then wolf. Got it."

Walker shook his head before kissing her. "You're so damn strong."

"I don't feel like that every day."

"Then I'll make sure you do." And when he kissed her again, she knew there would be no stopping—not that she wanted him to.

He led her to his bedroom, and for that she was grateful. She was nervous enough right then, and she needed a bit of normalcy. Having sex on the couch wouldn't have done it for her right then. Not that she'd say that to him since that would definitely kill the mood.

"Slow again?" he whispered against her lips, and she couldn't help but smile.

"We didn't exactly go slow last time." Who was this woman speaking, and how had Aimee become her so quickly? She pushed those thoughts from her mind and arched into him.

They were standing in front of his bed, his body over hers as he leaned down. She wasn't that tall, and he was above average in height. Without him lowering his head, she could only kiss the bottom of his chin. He was the one who had to lower his head so they could kiss unless she got a stool—something that was not out of the realm of possibility. Of course, she had a feeling he wouldn't keep his head up and not bend down for her unless they were teasing.

And the idea that, after this, they could have time to tease and find out who they could be as a couple warmed her even as it sent butterflies fluttering in her stomach.

He traced her jaw with his finger, bringing her attention back to him and not what could happen next...what *would* happen next and after.

"I can't wait to memorize everything about you," he said softly. "To know every inch, to *taste* every inch."

She swallowed hard. "As long as I can do the same."

His grin went feral, and then he kissed her again, this time with so much heat, her toes curled, and she rocked into him. They were pressed so closely together that she could feel his arousal against her stomach, and she shivered. She'd already had him inside her once, yet this would be a new experience.

He cupped her face before sliding his hand around the back of her head to cup her nape through her hair. "Slow," he said once again. "I think slow will be good."

"You say slow, but..." She arched into him then let out a gasp as he slid his hand between them and covered her heat through her jeans.

"Fine, just a little bit faster." And when he kissed her again, there was more urgency, a spark that pushed them both farther and faster.

She tugged on his shirt, and he moved back, stripping it over his head without a second thought. When he helped her out of her clothes, she kept her lips on his chest, licking and sucking his skin as he palmed her bare breasts and slid his hands over the silkiness of her skin between her thighs.

When he let her take his jeans off, she wrapped her hand around him, enjoying his moan as she remembered what it felt like to have him inside her. And, soon, he would be again.

"You're already wet," he growled. "Just one touch, and you're wet for me."

"Only for you," she said, her words truth.

He wrapped his hand around hers and pumped, the action erotic as their eyes met. "You like holding me? Like bringing me to the edge? You're so damn hot when you touch me, Aimee. I could get lost in your touch forever." He stopped her hand and squeezed once, hard. It wasn't as hard as he could have given her with his strength, but the action stalled her movements, making her sway.

"If you keep touching me like that, I'll go too fast, and I don't want to wait. I know I said slow." He growled low. "I lied."

Then she was on her back, and his head was between her legs. She gripped the comforter, her mouth parting as he licked and sucked her lower lips. He teased her clit with his tongue before letting out another growl. The vibration went to her bundle of nerves and even deep inside her, though he'd kept his fingers carefully away from her opening, teasing her with his mouth alone. She came hard, calling his name, and soon, he was over her, capturing the rest of her scream with his mouth.

He kissed her hard, and she wrapped her arms around his back, her hands digging into his skin, needing more, aching for far more.

"I need you in me," she whispered. "Now."

He kissed her jaw, his cock teasing her entrance. "Patience, Aimee."

She bit his jaw in turn. "Walker."

"You know biting only turns a wolf on."

"Next time, I'm going to suck on those pretty nipples until you come from just my touch, then I'm going to eat you until you come again, and then I want you to ride me, that way, I can play with your wet and sore nipples more. What do you say, Aimee? Will you ride me?"

She opened her mouth to speak, but couldn't when he flicked his finger over her clit.

But he stopped teasing her and, thankfully, *thankfully*, he slid deep inside, stretching her with this length. Her body shook, and they both broke out in a sweat as they moved together. He slid in and out of her, his gaze never leaving hers. With each thrust, she was closer and closer to coming, but she kept hanging on, not wanting to go until he did.

And though the first time they were together had been singularly the most sensual and *perfect* experience of her life, this...this was *more*.

Maybe it was intent. Maybe it was because she knew what could happen. But this was...different.

"Aimee. *Mine*."

"Mine," she repeated, and then she came, Walker doing the same as he kissed her hard before ripping his mouth from hers. Fangs elongated from his gums, but she wasn't scared.

This was Walker.

Healer. Wolf. Man.

Hers.

Hers.

Walker bit into her shoulder, and she cried out, not in pain, but in pleasure as the sensation sent her over the edge into another orgasm. As soon as his lips touched her shoulder, his mouth holding her steady, something inside her snapped into place.

Warmth spread through her chest, and she could see, could *feel*, a thread wrapping around her heart and soul, the other end tying her to Walker. Something pulsed deeply inside her, her body feeling as though there were a million tiny pinpricks of sensation bursting and vibrating all over her skin at the same time.

Walker, *her mate*, let go of her shoulder, licking the mark before letting out a growl. He took her lips, and though she could taste her own blood, it wasn't weird, not in this way, not in this moment. He was a wolf, and she was *his*.

They were cemented together in time at that moment, their bodies one as the mating bond slid into place. Another bond, this one not as warm and bright but just as steady, closed around her, and she knew that was the tie to the Pack.

She was a Talon. She was Walker's.

She wasn't the Aimee she'd been a few moments ago, wasn't the woman she was a month ago.

She was new, with a future path to forge.

And while it should have scared her, she could only relish it and hold Walker closer.

Walker was her mate. Now, she had to figure out what that meant. She'd known she could fall for this man, could love him with every ounce of her being, and now that she'd taken this step, she knew she could let herself fall for him—something she'd tried not to do initially because of the odds stacked against them.

She let out a sigh as Walker held her close, murmuring

sweet words to her. There would be times to come where they could figure out what to do next, but for now, she would sink into his hold and forget the rest of the world.

Because if she didn't do that? Well...the world wouldn't forget her so easily, would it?

"It feels so weird," Aimee said then frowned. "That's not the right word."

"Weird is as good a word as any since it's so new," Walker said, his voice warm. She could *feel* him inside her with such intensity it sometimes scared her. Yet at other times over the past few hours, it was as if nothing had changed. Their mating bond was still finding a way to settle and, apparently, it would do this oscillating thing for a little while longer.

He squeezed her hand as they walked along one of the paths that led out of the Talon Pack den and into the forest surrounding it. According to Walker, they were still on Talon territory, but not inside the actual wards. She didn't quite understand the difference, other than the fact that one had more guards than the other, but she would learn.

Because, apparently, she was a Talon member now.

Oh, boy.

Other than not needing to stand next to Walker when

she went through the wards, nothing had changed too much in the past few hours. They hadn't spoken to any other member of the Pack yet since they'd wanted to just be by themselves while they figured out this new normal but, apparently, Gideon had texted Walker to welcome her to the Pack.

There would be more formal things later, but for now, it was just the two of them.

What *formal things* would there be for two people who were now mated but only in the beginning stages of their relationship? They didn't love one another. Oh, there were sparks and perhaps the beginnings of what could be love, but they'd done all of this in the wrong order. She just hoped Walker didn't feel as though he made a mistake.

"You're thinking too hard," he said, not looking at her.

"This is awkward, I can't help it."

He frowned, stopped walking, and this time, turned to fully face her. "What's awkward?"

She waved her hand around in the air. "This. All of this. We're *mates,* and I have no idea what I'm supposed to say or feel. I mean, I probably wouldn't feel this way if we'd known each other and dated for years and slowly eased into mating. But since we didn't, I not only have my normal anxiety, I have the newness added on." She met his gaze, making sure he saw the intent in her eyes. "I am *not* regretting. I'm just saying...we did things backwards, and I'm going to need some time—with *you*—to make sure we don't forget any of the steps we skipped."

Walker was quiet for so long, she was afraid she'd said something wrong, but then he smiled widely, and she moved that much closer to being in love with him. He had a truly beautiful smile with the barest hint of a dimple that did warm things to her, and she couldn't help but smile back.

"You sound pretty normal to me." He paused, cupping her face. "We're going to make this work. Not because of what Avery said, but because of what *we* want."

"I believe in you. In what we can *be*. I never believed in anything before, not really. So we might be doing this backwards..."

"But we're still doing this," he finished for her.

He kissed her softly, the mating bond between them flaring so it warmed her, but it didn't scare her like it might have just an hour ago. She was far more resilient than she'd given herself credit for in the past.

"How about we play twenty questions?" Walker asked. "That's still a thing, right? It was when I was a kid, at least."

She snorted. "You're not *that* much older than me."

"Almost a century," he said, and while it should have

sounded weird, it was their new normal. It had been a different normal even before their mating as she had already been immersed into the paranormal world with Dawn and getting to know the wolves through her friends. Her *normal* hadn't been like others for longer than meeting Walker. "But that kind of age difference doesn't really matter once everyone starts aging like us."

"Okay, so twenty questions," she said quickly, doing her best not to think about wolves and what her next phase would be. They hadn't talked about when she would change, but she knew the conversation was looming. From the way she'd felt when she walked through the wards, they'd all known the curse was still active. There was no hiding from it. When everything settled down inside her, and Walker was able to test the bonds between them, they would start the process of seeing if she could be Healed.

All of this could be for naught, though, and that idea scared her. So, she didn't think about it. *One step at a time*, she reminded herself. One freakishly large step at a time.

"I'll go first. What's the order of the triplets? I actually don't know who is older." She blushed, knowing she should have known at least *that* before she mated Walker, but there was no going back now."

Walker smiled. "It goes Kameron, then me, then Brandon. I'm the middle child of the triplets and, apparently, acted like it."

She wasn't sure she quite believed that since all of the Brentwoods seemed to care for one another as if they were all the eldest siblings. It was something—a true strength—she'd admired even before she knew Walker was hers.

"What about your family? I don't know much about them."

"My parents worked their tails off at dead-end jobs that usually amounted to nothing. My cousins and the rest of the family are pretty much the same way. No matter how hard we try, the family can't save a dime. Stock market crashes, bad investments, literal thieves. My family has seen it all. No one has been to college in generations, though none of us are dumb, we just can't afford it, and life keeps getting in the way. I know my great-grandparents had a decent nest egg, and even had degrees, but other than that...nothing."

Walker frowned at her. "You know, it could be that your *line* is cursed, not just you. And the curse is reacting differently to you than it did with the others."

Aimee had no idea what to think about that, or what she was going to say, because as soon as she opened her mouth to speak, Walker's head shot up, and he pulled her behind him.

A beautiful woman with long, blond hair and a fierce

strength in the way she walked—no *prowled*—toward them slid through the trees. She inclined her head at them but didn't stop moving.

"Walker, right?" the stranger asked, and Aimee had the sudden urge to rake her nails down her mate's arm and show the world who he belonged to.

She must have made a noise, or Walker felt her emotions through the bond because he gave her an approving look before looking back at the other woman.

"Audrey, good to see you. Are you alone?"

Audrey nodded. "Yes." She gave Aimee a pointed look that got her hackles up. Apparently, Aimee was now not only territorial when it came to her new mate, but also acting more wolf-like with every passing moment.

"Aimee, this is Audrey, Beta of the Aspen Pack. Audrey, this is my mate, Aimee."

Audrey gave Walker a look before nodding at Aimee. "You smell of him, but I couldn't be sure. Congratulations on your new mating. I assume it's new since you weren't mated the last time I saw you."

"Yes, and thank you," Walker said. "Are you here for a reason?" Aimee had a feeling he was being careful with his words, and she didn't blame him as they weren't in den territory, and anyone could overhear.

Suddenly, Aimee didn't feel as safe anymore.

The other woman nodded, then looked sharply at

Aimee. Before Aimee could ask what was wrong, she called out, her back bending back as a shocking pain slammed into her. Blood poured out of her nose, and she fell forward, her limbs shaking, her hands clamping down hard.

Walker caught her in his arms and yelled her name, but she couldn't really hear him.

Audrey was by her side, as well, holding her arm as if she were trying to help, but Aimee didn't understand what was going on. She didn't know anything it seemed.

Had they been too late, after all?

No matter the bond, no matter the visions from Avery, they had lost.

The curse had won.

And now, Aimee would lose Walker...and herself. Forever.

CHAPTER 11

WALKER'S WOLF pushed at him, wanting to claw anyone who got too near, but he knew it wouldn't help a damn thing. *He* couldn't change a damn thing. He was a Healer who couldn't Heal the one person who mattered the most, and until the end of his days, he would never forget the sound that Aimee made as she fell, never forget the shock on her face as the truth of what was happening settled over both of them.

He was about to lose his mate before he even truly had her.

And he had no way of stopping it, not anymore, not even with the strength in his body—the horror of the curse far darker than anything he'd seen before. Because of their fragile and far-too-new mating bond, he could feel her terror and agony, or at least her reaction to them as she seized on the ground in front of him.

He tried to push his magic through their bond as Pack and mates, but it only slid over her like a blanket, not penetrating but at least easing *some* of her pain.

Though not enough.

It would never be enough.

He would never be enough.

Walker met the gold of Audrey's gaze and growled. "I can't help her."

His Healing did nothing, even as he tried over and over to do *something* to save his mate. Their bond pulsed, warming before going back to its resting state, as if it couldn't handle any more than it already had.

Audrey let out a breath. "She's dying, I can smell it on her."

He let out a growl, low and deadly. "She. Can't. Die."

The lion shifter didn't back down. Instead, she met his eyes, the dominance there almost making him drop his gaze, though he didn't, not when Aimee was lying beside him in pain. He couldn't show weakness, not in front of this near stranger.

"Can we move her to your clinic? Take her to your Alpha? Because she won't last much longer as a human. She has to be changed."

He'd come to that same conclusion, but he hadn't

wanted to voice that, not yet. Not when he and Aimee hadn't been able to discuss it. He would *never* change another without their consent, and though they'd talked about her becoming a wolf soon, he still needed to hear her voice.

Or, perhaps, he needed to hear her voice because once he did, he would know she would be okay.

Only nothing would be okay.

"We don't have time," he growled as he put his hand on her pulse. It was thready, and he knew that if they didn't move soon, they wouldn't have time to make *any* decisions. Her body had stilled, forcing his wolf to lash out at him, trying to figure out a way to save their mate. "If we don't change her now, we won't be able to later."

Audrey's eyes widened. "She's your mate, so I assume that you both knew she would one day become a wolf?"

He nodded. "We're so damn new. She was supposed to have more time." *They* were supposed to have more time. His wolf tugged at him, but he knew he wouldn't be enough.

In order to change a human into a wolf—and perhaps *any* shifter since he didn't know about the other type well enough—the human had to be near death. A single bite or slash wouldn't do it. They had to be mauled, sliced up, and bitten to the point of agony and then, only then, would the wolf rise to the surface to allow whatever was in the bite to form a new shifter. It was an excruciating process that didn't necessarily work in all cases, and almost always required the bite of an Alpha or a shifter that was nearly as dominant.

Someone far more dominant than Walker.

Tears burned at the backs of his eyes, but he pushed them away. There would be time for self-recrimination and sorrow later. Aimee didn't have enough time left for him to beat himself up for not being dominant enough to save her.

"I'm not dominant enough." His words were hollow, though every emotion that dared slide through his system barreled into his heart and soul. He was showing weakness to someone he didn't know because there was nothing else he could do. Aimee was no longer screaming, and her heartbeat was slowing.

They were far enough away from the den that the sentries couldn't hear them, not where they were. He could call Mitchell, Gideon, or even Ryder to him, but he didn't know if they were even in the den. All of them had prior commitments that day in order to help the Pack.

Walker was alone in his dawning horror.

Except there was one other near him who was far more dominant. Another who could help. But in so doing, it could threaten so much more than what they might gain by giving Aimee more time. It would be selfish, and not something he could demand.

But he could ask.

"Audrey..."

"I...if I do this, Blade will *know* I told you about the existence of cat shifters. There will be no hiding it. And since she is already a Talon, she will be the lone feline in a Pack full of wolves. Things won't be easy for her, and you will *have* to hide what she is from the humans. We're out of satellite range right now, but no matter what happens next, you *must* protect the secret. I told you and the rest of your family what I am because the moon goddess insisted." She cursed under her breath. "This might be the reason for her telling me to do so, and I hate that it is."

"I can't force you to do this, I can only ask and try to make you understand that I have nothing else. She's my everything." At least she would be, or maybe she already was. He needed more time to figure that out. He hadn't known that was true until the words slipped from his mouth, but he knew now that deep in his gut it was.

Audrey's body shivered before she gave him a tight nod. "I'll need to shift to complete it, but I can bite her now to start the process. I pray to the moon goddess that not only this works, but that it's the right thing to do."

Her fangs elongated to about the same size his had when he marked Aimee the night before, but he knew this bite wouldn't be like the one he'd given. This one would *hurt*. It would eventually kill. And, hopefully, it would bring her back.

Audrey's eyes shifted, her pupils slit like a cat's. Her fangs were also curved differently, but it didn't change the sound of tearing flesh as Audrey bit into his mate's upper arm near her shoulder. It was far too close to the mating mark he had given Aimee the night before, but he couldn't stop the other woman as she worked. The Beta of the Aspen Pack was risking everything to save Aimee, and for that, Walker would forever be in her debt.

He just prayed his own Alpha—and Aimee—would forgive him.

His mate opened her mouth, a soundless scream escaping. He lowered his head, careful to stay out of Audrey's way, and pressed his lips to her forehead, trying with all his might to soothe her pain by using their bonds. It wasn't easy during a forced change, and a rare occurrence since most wolves mated other wolves, but he'd be damned if he sat by and let her fall away from him in pain. Pain meds didn't work on shifters at the best of times, and adding them during a change interrupted the magic and usually ended up with the person in either far more painful shifts or dead. And it wasn't as though he had any pain meds to give her anyway. He might also be a doctor and had finished medical school twice over, but he didn't carry around a first-aid kit while walking around the Talon territory.

While he held Aimee close to him, Audrey pulled away and began stripping off her clothes. To ensure that enough of the enzyme that leaked from the fangs of a shifter as they bit entered the bloodstream and tissues, whoever was doing the changing needed to be in their animal form. He looked away from Audrey and let her shift with as much privacy as he could allow, but he could still hear the sounds of bones breaking and muscles tearing as she turned into her lioness form. She shifted far faster than most of the wolves he knew, and he had a feeling part of that was because she'd begun shifting while biting into Aimee the first time.

The golden lioness bit again, this time, her fangs sliding in deeper. Aimee was already near death, and with each bite, she slid further and further away from him.

"Jesus," Gideon said as he fell to his knees beside Walker. He put his hand on Walker's shoulder and fought to catch his breath. His brother must have run from wherever he'd been with Brie some distance away from the den in order to attempt to help.

As Alpha, Gideon wouldn't have needed a phone call to know what was going on, he'd have felt Aimee's distress through the Pack bonds and would have dropped everything to come to her aid.

That was the kind of Alpha Gideon was, and Walker hoped to the goddess that he forgave him for what was happening now.

"I can sense her through the bonds," Gideon said softly. "She's strong. She's fighting. And though Audrey is the one changing her, she'll still end up a Talon. She's *ours*, Walker. This wasn't how it was supposed to go, but we'll make it work."

Audrey let out a huff that sounded like she wanted to growl but couldn't at the moment, and Walker figured the cat agreed with Gideon. Audrey sat back after a moment, her muzzle red with Aimee's blood, and her eyes cat-gold. Walker stood abruptly, cradling an unconscious Aimee to his chest.

"I need to get her back to the clinic." Walker's arms were steady, but inside, he was shaking like a damn leaf.

"You need to go," Gideon growled low at Audrey. "We'll try to keep what she is as secret as possible, but Blade will eventually find out what you did." He paused. "Do you need sanctuary?"

She shook her head, though Walker knew from experience that the action wasn't easy in animal form. She gave Walker a slight nod, stared at Aimee for a few moments, then ran off in the opposite direction at full speed. Whatever she'd been coming to speak to Gideon about would now have to wait because she'd risked so much to save

Aimee. Walker would never forget that, nor would he stand back if Audrey were hurt because of what she'd done to try and save his mate.

"Come on," Gideon growled. "The others are on their way, and she needs to be in a safe place when she wakes up. You can tell me exactly what happened along the way."

Walker held Aimee closer, then started running full-tilt toward the den. Gideon would have been faster if he'd held Aimee, but with Walker's wolf so close to the surface, he knew he wouldn't have been able to allow that. They slid through the wards, and Aimee didn't react—not because the curse was gone, but because she was in the throes of whatever needed to happen in order for her to change. As much as he studied the science of it, he knew it was the magic of the moon goddess that carried most through the initial transformations.

They made it to the clinic, and Walker was aware that others in the Pack were staring at the tableau the three of them created. Their Alpha, sweaty and growling, his wolf clearly in his stride. Walker, covered in blood and far more aggressive than he usually was. And Aimee, lying prone in Walker's arms, also covered in blood and wounds.

The others would ask questions, and some would get the full story. Not everyone could be allowed to know who'd changed Aimee. It wasn't safe for Audrey, and though it killed him that he couldn't trust every single member of his Pack, they had been betrayed one too many times. It was also safer for them if they didn't know every secret that could get them hurt. The Pack wasn't a democracy, and that was something the newer wolves and Pack members had a harder time figuring out.

"What do you need?" Gideon asked.

"Leah. Bring Leah." He knew his wolf was in his voice, and he was barely able to get the words out, but his brother understood.

Walker stripped Aimee out of her torn and bloody clothing, his hands shaking. He covered her with a blanket as he washed her wounds, the fact that they were already starting to heal settling him only for a brief moment. They still weren't out of the woods.

If he hadn't seen Audrey doing her best to start the shift, he'd have thought his mate dead. It was only seeing that and feeling the mating bond that kept him from going wolf and attacking anything that came near. For a wolf who claimed he wasn't as dominant as others, he was acting like Kameron or Mitchell just then, rather than the laid-back one he usually was.

He supposed mating did that to a person.

Almost losing a mate only made it worse.

He cupped her face, leaning down so he was only a

breath away from her. "I'm so damn sorry. So fucking sorry."

The others of his family came into the room then, their quiet footsteps almost in mourning as they gathered around him. Leah stood the closest to him, her mate Ryder behind her.

"What can I do?" she asked, her voice soft.

"Help watch her wounds to be sure they're healing," he said roughly. He didn't know if it was because of his wolf or the fact that tears were clogging his throat.

Brie came to his other side and put her hand on his back. Immediately, he relaxed. She wasn't an Omega, but she *was* a submissive wolf who could calm his wolf with her mere presence. Brandon would be able to do that, as well, but Walker wasn't sure if his wolf would allow that just then. His other half couldn't help but want to protect Brie, so it calmed him enough for Walker to be able to think through the clouds of fear and pain circling in his mind.

"She'll be a lion then?" Kameron asked, his voice soft. "What are we going to do with that information?"

"What do you mean?" Brynn asked. She and her mate Finn had apparently been in the den when the call went out and had now joined his *entire* family, mates and all, in the small room. They weren't going to let him be alone. They weren't going to allow Aimee to be alone.

"He means, will we let the Pack know she's a cat," Walker growled out. "She won't smell like a wolf, but we all know that even though Audrey doesn't smell like us, she still smells like a shifter."

Kameron rubbed a hand over his face. Walker only saw this because his brother had moved to the opposite end of the bed where he frowned down at Aimee's form. Walker wasn't sure he liked so many watching his mate while she was in such a weak state, but he knew they were there for support, not judgment.

"We won't be able to hide her from the Pack," Gideon said after a moment. "And it would be a disservice to Aimee to do so, I would think. But we will have to think about how we explain the *why* of it. Audrey risked a lot for us. Hell, she might have risked everything. Once Blade finds out that we have a new lion in our Pack, he'll discover who made her. We don't know how many cats or even other shifter types they have in the Aspens, but only one that *we* know of is able to make another shifter. Only one lion dominant enough to make it happen. We're already on the brink of something far greater than us, yet I think we're only seeing the tip of the iceberg when it comes to Blade's secrets."

They were all quiet as they digested the information. Once again, their Pack and their people would be changed. Somehow, they would have to come together to determine the next steps.

"I need to call Dhani and Cheyenne," Dawn said softly into the silence from the other side of the room. "The four of us promised we'd never keep secrets from each other again. I know they aren't Pack, but..."

Gideon let out a sigh. "The four of you are a special circumstance, and we all know it. There's a reason you were a group before this, and a reason two of the four of you are now mated into the Pack. Bring them in. We'll tell them. They need to know about her now anyway." He sighed. "What we tell them about Audrey, however, is another matter."

"I won't tell them who changed Aimee," Dawn said quickly. "There are some things that are Pack need-to-know only, but one of us turning into a shifter isn't something I think we can feasibly hide."

Walker listened with half an ear as the others discussed the logistics and potential pitfalls of what would happen when—not if, but *when*—Aimee woke up and found herself a lion. Walker only knew about big cats in the wild from watching nature shows. He didn't know anything about how they hunted or how he would need to Heal them in animal form. He didn't know what the differences between a shifter and a wild lion were. But he would learn. He'd find anything he could. Even though the elders had never heard of cat shifters until recently, he would learn.

For Aimee, he would learn.

He closed his eyes and wrapped himself around their bond, needing to know that she would be his in truth, that she would survive this.

And that's when it happened.

The bond settled between them, even through her fading pain. And he could sense the curse.

The fucking curse that had killed her.

"Holy shit," he whispered.

"I feel it, too," Leah said softly from his side. "I can ease the ache with my magic, using the water within her body to cool any heat that will come from breaking the curse. And if someone gets me two basins of water on either side of me, I can work with that, as well." She was a water witch, and her healing came from her element as well as the magic within her body.

"It's from a witch, though," he said. "I can taste it."

"If we don't take care of it now, I don't know if we will see it again," Leah added. "Because she's in the middle of a change like this, it's making the curse more...raw for lack of a better word."

"If we don't break it now, even when she's unconscious and still in pain, I don't know if we will get the chance to do it again. Ever."

Walker met Leah's gaze and knew the grief in her eyes matched his own. If they didn't break the curse, it wouldn't matter if Aimee was a cat or not, she'd still fade.

And he refused to let that happen.

The others muttered around them as they discussed what that meant and the why of it, but Walker couldn't focus on that right then. He had to keep his mind on the curse wrapped around his mate like a tightening barbed web.

"I can't tell what kind of witch did this, but the magic isn't water. Air, maybe? I know it's not fire, though, it doesn't burn."

If it wasn't a fire witch, it couldn't be the red witch that Blade employed. What that meant in the grand scheme of things, he didn't know, but he would focus on it later.

After he broke the curse.

"I might need your strength," he whispered, knowing Gideon would hear him.

"You have it."

"You have all of our strength," Parker said. "You both saved me, I won't let another witch hurt us."

"Watch your tone about witches," Ryder warned.

"He didn't mean it that way," Brandon interjected.

"Shut up," Max growled. "She needs us."

His cousin's surprising words broke through the

tension, and Walker breathed in the power that was his family, his Pack, and *Healed*. His magic wrapped around each strand of the curse, encircling the tiny threads and spiraling around them. Sweat poured down his face and back as he worked. What he was doing was at the far edges of his abilities, but with Leah gently soothing the fractured connections as he worked, he was able to slowly maneuver around each of the threads that encased Aimee before he let out a deep breath.

"Ready?" he asked, his voice hoarse.

"Yes." Leah's answer sounded far away, but he knew she leaned against her mate, using his strength to prop herself up so she could lend her energy to Aimee.

He didn't know if it would work, but he had to try. Had to hope, and to pray.

The room heated to the point of near pain, and then it was as if something in a vacuum popped.

He fell back, and if it weren't for Kameron and Gideon propping him up, he'd have landed on the floor. He had no more energy left and couldn't even open his eyes to see his mate, but he could *feel* her.

The others would know what to do next, but for now, he would lean on his family and know that his mate was safe.

She was his. She was Pack. She was a shifter.

And she was *Healed*.

CHAPTER 12

FALLING.

She was falling.

That was the one thing Aimee knew for sure. Though even as she thought it, she knew she was mistaken. Falling wasn't quite right. Because if she were, she wouldn't feel as if she had already landed.

How could she be plummeting and ripped from landing at the same time?

And why was she so focused on the terms when there was a new presence warming her. Not the cord that wrapped its way around her soul, warm and aching as it reached for her, protective and circling as it prowled. That one felt as if it had always been there, merely waiting under veiled secrecy for her to find.

This new entity wasn't a bond like the other.

No, this was something new, something...small and frightened even as it hovered and protected.

Perhaps this was how she would exist in her afterlife. She would spend her time wondering what things were and how to describe them.

For Aimee had died, she remembered it. Remembered falling against Walker and crying out in pain as the end rushed in. She didn't remember living, but she remembered dying.

The new warmth she didn't quite understand cuddled closer, nudging her as it curled into a ball near her and purred.

Purred.

As if it were a kitten.

The kitten, or whatever this warmth was, nudged her again, this time nipping gently at her fingers. The nipping increased to a dull pinprick, and before she could wonder what was going on...she woke up.

The light above her blinded her, but she didn't keep her eyes shut. Instead, she blinked a few times and wondered where she was. One moment, she was screaming; the next, she was in the abyss. Now, what was happening?

Warmth over her skin below her elbow.

Breath on her cheek as she blinked her eyes open once again.

"Aimee."

Walker.

Her mate.

Hers.

His face filled her vision, and he cupped her cheek. There were tears in his eyes, and his beard had grown in as if he hadn't trimmed it in days. How long had she been...asleep? Was that the word she should use?

"Aimee." This time, his voice broke, and she lifted her hand up to cup the back of his head, petting him through his hair. It wasn't until the soft strands slid through her fingers that she realized that she'd been able to do that with no pain at all. It hadn't taken any strength to lift her arm, while it probably should have taken a lot considering it looked as if she'd been immobile for quite a while.

"What happened?" she asked. She licked her lips, her throat a bit dry, and Walker moved away from her and out of her line of sight. She made a small noise that didn't sound like anything she'd ever uttered before. It was more like the mew a kitten would make.

A kitten.

Why was that fact so important, and why had she thought of kittens *twice*?

Walker fiddled with something below the bed she was on, and it moved so she could sit up. She must be in Walker's clinic, and this was one of his hospital beds. "Here, take a few sips of water. Your throat has to be dry." He held out a small cup with a straw, and she sucked cold water between her lips, a sigh escaping as she drank as quickly as Walker allowed her to.

"Thank you," she whispered. "What happened?" she asked again. She knew there were other things to ask, other senses she should be using so she could fully look at the world around her, but right then, her world narrowed to Walker and what he would say next.

She told herself to start small, then look left. Look right. Look behind. Perhaps then, look forward.

Since she was now positioned so she could meet his gaze, Walker sat next to her on the bed and cupped her cheek once more. The action tangled the tips of his fingers in her hair, and she leaned into his touch, breathing him in. Their mating bond pulsated, and she reveled in that connection.

The fact that she could feel this strongly about someone so quickly just told her that their circumstances and who they *were* alone and as a couple were what made what they had work. She was falling for him, and from his touch alone, she knew it was *right*. She didn't know what had led her to be in this room and to feel so...*different*, but she knew the reason she was able to hold Walker close at all because he was *hers*.

"You had a seizure when the curse fluxed again while

we were out for a walk beyond the wards. Audrey was with us. Remember?"

She nodded, the details slowly falling into place. She remembered everything up to her fall, but she had a feeling her mind was protecting her from everything that came after.

"I remember," she said.

"It was bad this time, baby," he whispered. He'd never called her *baby* before, and she knew the endearment meant that something more than bad had happened. Something he was trying to ease into. "Whatever Avery saw, it all came to this. You weren't going to make it unless we did something to save you, and no amount of my Healing would have worked." She knew that must have hurt him to reveal, as he hated feeling weak. Yet he'd said his Healing hadn't worked.

So what had?

Something inside her warmed, uncurling as it had curled within her earlier.

"Walker, how am I here if you couldn't Heal me?"

"We had to change you. To bite you." Her world froze before it thawed just as quickly when she looked at the worry in his gaze. "I know the plan was for you to change eventually, and even before this, we were rushing into all these decisions, but if we didn't do what we did when we did it, I would have lost you."

Aimee let out a long breath and looked down at her hands, trying to focus on what to say. Was that what the warmth was? Her wolf? She only had a vague idea of what it meant to be changed into a shifter. It hadn't been something in her world before the Unveiling, and even after she'd found out that one of her best friends was a wolf, she hadn't thought about the process of someone changing from human to shifter. Dawn had been born a wolf, and even then, Aimee didn't know the details of when the shifting started or even what it actually meant to have an animal inside her.

Maybe once it actually hit her, she'd freak out. She'd ask for the details of how it had been done and why she had no scars on her hands from when she'd cut herself in the kitchen, or why that burn she'd gotten at the diner a couple of years ago was now gone.

She'd ask about what all of this new mythology meant and perhaps who she could be if the old Aimee were no longer part of her anymore. But, first, she needed to look into Walker's eyes and tell him this wasn't on him.

This wasn't his fault.

She couldn't blame him for what had happened to her, even if she wasn't sure she was *herself* anymore at all.

"I'm a wolf now?" she asked. Because who was she without these answers? Though why she was going through an existential crisis as she sat on a hospital bed in Walker's arms, she didn't know.

A pained look crossed Walker's face, and she frowned, the action hurting her head for some reason. Everything was so new, so fresh, that things like new facial expressions hurt just a little.

"I'm not dominant enough to change someone into a wolf. You need to be an Alpha or at a power one or two steps right below that in the hierarchy. If we'd been alone, I don't know if I would have been fast enough to get you back to the den and to Ryder or Mitchell or Gideon. I wouldn't have been enough."

There was something she should have said to soothe him then since that was what she did, alleviate others' worries because it helped her breathe, but she couldn't think of it.

"I'm confused." She took a deep breath and rubbed her temple, vaguely aware that all those aches and pains she'd had before were now gone. Was that the wolf? Or was she able to ignore her curse now?

"Audrey had to change you, Aimee. And she's...she's not a wolf. None of us knew they even existed, but there are other things out in the world beyond wolves and witches. You won't shift into a wolf. You'll be a Talon, but you won't be a wolf like I am."

The kitten purred.

Was that important, or was she still dreaming?

And why did that kitten keep coming to her mind?

Her breath came in rapid pants, and she tried to understand what was going on. "What...what does Audrey change into?" *What will I turn into?*

Walker cupped her face with both hands. "She's a lion. And soon, you'll shift into a lioness, as well." He let out a rough chuckle. "Hell, Aimee, I never thought this would be a conversation I'd ever have. But you're going to be okay. Between Audrey changing you, and us getting you back in time to Heal what we could, you're going to be okay. The cat will do the rest."

Aimee blinked a few times, her mind trying to catch up with Walker's words even as she tried to figure out if she actually felt any differently than she had before she was on that field with Walker.

"I...I think I'm going to be...not sick...but I think I'm dizzy." Not the most eloquent thing to say, nor was it something that made sense because while she was dizzy, she also knew there wasn't anything Walker could do about it.

Proving that she was so far out of her depth regarding everything non-human, Walker frowned before rubbing his thumbs over her temples.

"I can feel your slight headache, and I think that has more to do with all this information being tossed at you at once than from you hitting your head. But let me take care of it for you."

Her chest warmed as what she now knew were bonds flared between them, and soon, her headache was gone, and she was staring into Walker's eyes.

"It doesn't hurt you when you do that?" she asked, worried. "You don't need to take in my pain or anything in order to Heal?"

He shook his head. "Only in rare instances does that happen, and it's usually because of magic, not because of an actual injury."

"Thank you," she whispered. "Thank you for taking care of my headache because you didn't want to see me in pain, and thank you for saving my life." She let out a breath. "And...I guess I need to find Audrey and thank her, as well. A lion? Like an actual lion?"

Of all the things she'd have thought might come into her life one day, turning into a lion was *never* one of them. Honestly, the only dream she'd ever had for her future was to actually have one. This was so far out of her sphere that it was almost comical.

Walker's lips quirked into a smile, and she couldn't help but think that he looked so much less weary when he smiled. She loved the way he looked with any expression on his face, but him smiling was her favorite. Or maybe it was that dark look in his eyes right before he entered her.

She sucked in a breath at that thought, and Walker's eyes went dark as soon as the thoughts entered her mind. For some reason, she could scent a warm, almost cinnamon-like smell in the air, and she sucked in a breath at how...turned on that made her.

"Good to know you still want me," he whispered, kissing her lips gently.

She blushed. "You can tell just by my face?"

"And I can scent it, but then again, I suppose you can now, too." He kissed her again before letting out a sigh and pulling back. "That will have to wait though because we have a few things to talk about, and I don't want to get distracted with how much I want you."

Hell, this would take a lot of getting used to, but first, she needed to get the rest of the story from him because she honestly had no idea what she was doing.

"Okay," she said after a moment, clearing her throat.

"I had this whole thing planned out where I was going to tell you our history and then walk you into what you could expect and then even take you home so you could sleep in your bed. Now, I'm thinking that I'll have to go into professor mode and bore the hell out of you when you probably had questions for me."

She couldn't help but smile at him, he was so damned *caring*, and he wanted to do the best for others. No wonder the Pack ran him ragged most days, even when they didn't realize they were doing it. Walker couldn't say no to helping others—even her—and now that she was his, she knew that it would be a part of her duty as his mate to ensure that he took care of himself, as well.

"Why don't you go through your list and I'll ask questions as we go along? Because I feel like I'm in the *Twilight Zone* right now, and facts would probably help me." She'd been a waitress without any plans for the future not too long ago. Now, she was in such a new situation that going though things on a checklist would probably center her. Or scare the hell out of her. Either way, the more facts she had, the better. Right?

"Okay, then. Here we go. So, what do you know about where shifters come from?" he asked, settling in next to her so they were still facing each other but able to touch. She *needed* his touch, and had a feeling he felt the same.

"Let's go with the idea that I know nothing." Because that wasn't far from the truth.

"Once, before there were cities and tools beyond spears and rocks, there was a hunter. The first hunter. He killed a wolf on a hunt but did it out of rage, or perhaps it was something else that rode him. Regardless, it wasn't hunger that drove him at the time of the kill. The hunter would have eventually used the wolf to feed his family, perhaps, but in the heat of the moment, he let the hunt overtake him. The moon goddess saw this and stepped into the mortal realm, angered that the human would do that to a wolf. In punishment, she forced the soul of the wolf into the man and made them one. Two souls. One body. Two shapes. The man became the first shifter, and in turn, he changed two more men into wolves." He paused. "One day, I'll explain how those men and the first hunter are related to the Talons, but that's a lot of information for right now."

Confused but wanting to hear the end of the story, she nodded. "Okay."

"From there came the Packs and the hierarchies we have. We aren't forced to change under the moonlight, but when the moon calls, we *do* tend to change and run as a Pack. Any children that come from a mating will be wolves, though those children won't be able to change until they are two or three. Fallon being the exception since she's the future Alpha and changed *way* early." Walker cleared his throat. "Wolves have heightened senses, are fast, require *a lot* of food in order to maintain their energy, and are fiercely loyal even when it takes more...finesse to handle our tempers. We're all of those things and more." He leaned forward and pressed his forehead to hers before sitting back up so he could meet her gaze. "I honestly have no idea about cat shifters. I've only really seen Audrey change twice, and I wasn't paying attention to the process either time. I don't know their history, or what we will need to do so you can bond with your inner cat and find a way to *be*. But like I said, we'll learn."

"Can you ask Audrey?" She wasn't sure how she felt about the fact that she'd once again be the odd one out when it came to those around her. She'd always been the off one in her group of friends—or at least that's how she'd felt. She hadn't known Dawn felt the same way until recently.

A pained look crossed Walker's face, and she stiffened. "We can't get ahold of Audrey at the moment, and her having more contact with us could be bad for her anyway."

"What do you mean?"

He let out a sigh. "I can explain more later, but know that she's the Beta of the Aspen Pack, and the Alpha, *her* Alpha, doesn't get along with us. To the point where we think he was the one who sent the witch after Parker." At her widened eyes, he nodded. "The Aspens have greater numbers than we do, and they're stronger than us because they haven't had to fight demons or other Packs—or themselves—in the past century like we have—or like the Redwoods have. Blade made sure that no one outside his Pack knew of the existence of other shifters. So much so that we only *just* learned about it, and not all the Pack knows." He squeezed her hand, and she tilted her head to study him.

"Does this mean I have to hide what I am? Or, I guess, what I will be?" She would if she had to in order to keep Walker and his family safe, but she wasn't sure if that was even possible.

He shook his head and kissed her softly. That made something inside her perk up, and she had a feeling it was the kitten that wasn't a kitten. This would take some getting used to.

"There will be no hiding what you are, I don't think. Not within the Pack. We're going to do our best to keep the fact that you're *any* type of shifter away from the humans, though."

"You aren't allowed to change humans, I remember that." She sat up straighter and squeezed his arm. "Are you going to get in trouble? Is Audrey?"

He shook his head. "As long as we keep the truth of what you are away from Blade, Audrey should be okay."

She knew there was more to it and hated that she'd put the other woman in this position. Audrey risked so much for her, and there was nothing Aimee could do. Yet.

"As for the humans? If they find out, no...not even then. You're my mate, and it's the loophole they allowed. And we're only listening to their rules to avoid conflict and because it hasn't come up. We don't change humans often without them being mated in anyway. If and when that time comes, we will do what's best for the Pack, human rules or not. But what we really need to hide from them is *what* you are. The world doesn't know about anything outside of shifters, and they don't know much about us either. We need to keep it that way."

"This isn't going to be easy," she said. "But I don't want to be the reason the Pack is hurting. I never did. If it weren't for my curse, I wouldn't have needed to put Audrey or you in danger at all. I hate this."

She froze after the last words had left her mouth, and she stared at the way Walker's eyes widened when she said it.

"The curse..." she whispered. "It's...it's different." She didn't know how she knew, but there was something altered about the way she felt other than this new warmth growing inside her that nudged her as if petting and then curling up into a ball. She wasn't as weak as she had been before, and she had a feeling it wasn't because of what she'd become, but rather what was now gone.

"It's gone, Aimee." He kissed her hard, his eyes shiny. The stark emotion on his face made her fall that much more for him. If he weren't careful, she'd love him with every ounce of her being.

"How? What? When?" She couldn't seem to get her thoughts in order, and she was rambling.

"When we brought you back to the clinic, Leah and I were *finally* able to see the curse." His body shuddered, and she shifted over so she could wrap her arms around him. Her inner warmth—her cat—nudged her, and she could feel *his* wolf butt against him. It was as if their connection was now multi-layered, and this touch alone centered them both.

He swallowed hard, and she could feel it even though she couldn't see his face. "We knew if we didn't use our strengths to break the curse when your body was in flux and the magic stronger than ever, we might never get another chance. In doing so, the curse is *gone,* and you're going to be okay. But that doesn't mean it's over."

She pulled away and looked at him, his eyes gold. Would her eyes do the same one day? "I can't believe it."

She'd spent so long knowing her time was limited, that no matter how many doctors she went to, the bruises would be worse and her energy would deplete to almost nothing. Then she'd met Walker, and he'd figured it out.

"We're going to find out who did this to you, and Leah already has some clues for us. We're going to get to the bottom of this, Aimee, and when we do, we're going to figure out *why.*"

She cupped his face. "Thank you," she said softly. "Thank you for giving me...time. And you. Thank you for giving me *you.*"

"Always," he whispered against her mouth. "Always, Aimee."

Everything had once again shifted so far off its axis it barely resembled what it used to be, but she wasn't the weak one any longer. She could fight, and she would.

She wasn't the one to pity, the one to watch out for because she could fall and never return.

And when everything in her mind and soul finally settled down, she'd figure out what to do with all of that, because in the end, she wasn't the same Aimee she had been even a day ago.

Once again, she'd have to figure out this new Aimee.

But this time, she wouldn't be alone.

CHAPTER 13

WALKER KNEW his world had changed the day he met Aimee on that field in front of the Central den, but he hadn't known the breadth of it until he stood beside her, surrounded by wolves as she rolled her shoulders back and proved that her inner strength was far superior to anything she might have thought she possessed.

He hadn't known that his world would change with each and every breath and decision that they made.

He should have, though, especially knowing the moon goddess and how everything recently seemed beyond significant. He should have.

The problem he was having now, however, wasn't something he could handle with growling or even fierce looks.

His mate was a cat surrounded by wolves in a Pack

where most had never met a cat shifter. He wasn't sure what they would do if they were left to their own curiosities. As it was, Walker didn't know what aspects of her cat would show up in Aimee as some of his wolf ended up in his own personality. He was afraid those in the Pack who were already fearful or on edge with everything that had gone on in the past couple of years might do something they would regret.

Aimee slid her hand into his and frowned up at him. He cleared his throat and did his best to look like he wasn't stressed out with so many wolves staring at them as they walked through the middle of the den, but from the look on her face, he wasn't doing a good job of it.

"What's wrong?" she asked and stopped in the middle of the path on their way from his place to Gideon's. They had been summoned for a family meal and a small Pack meeting to discuss the thousand things going on around them—things that included Aimee. He and Aimee hadn't actually had a discussion about what their future would be beyond the fact that they were both relieved they would actually have one. He knew they needed to talk about the details like where she would live, what she would do within the Pack walls, or if they needed to be outside of them for her to be comfortable. The only real problem was that, since he was the Healer, he *needed* to live and work inside the den. If he and Aimee were mates, they had to do it together.

Creating a bond and making decisions that would change their lives forever had gotten in the way of talking about the small things that would make their lives together. And now he was so far inside his head, he was missing the big picture—something he'd done in the past worrying about everything he couldn't fix, couldn't Heal.

"Everything's fine," he said, knowing it wasn't quite the truth.

She gave him a look that told him she clearly didn't believe him, but before she could say anything, one of his wolves walked past them, his nostrils flaring as he sniffed in Aimee's direction before frowning.

The bond between him and Aimee was far too new for an unmated male to be so close to them, and for whatever thoughts went through the other man's mind as he tried to figure out what was off about Aimee's scent. Walker couldn't help the growl that escaped his lips.

The other wolf, Allen, immediately lowered his head. Allen was a dominant, but he was still slightly lower in rank than Walker. "Sorry, Walker. Didn't mean to offend. I know the mating bond is new, I just thought Aimee was human. Didn't know that had changed, and it's not my business I guess. That's all."

Walker forced himself to calm down since Allen

hadn't done anything wrong except be a little too curious. If Walker weren't careful, he'd start a dominance fight that he didn't want to be in the middle of since he already had enough to deal with. Plus, he was their Healer and had no right forcing others weaker than he was into any position they wouldn't feel comfortable in.

Walker inclined his head, knowing his wolf was far too jumpy to use his words at the moment. The other man graciously bowed his head again before walking away, leaving Aimee and Walker alone on the path once more. There were others around them, he could feel them watching, their gazes intent on Aimee—or rather pointedly anywhere *but* on Aimee. They might have stared blatantly at her before, but with his little show, they were doing their best not to. How could he blame them for their curiosity, though? She didn't smell like a wolf, nor did she smell human, not any longer. And it wasn't as if their Pack were that big. They'd known that Aimee, Cheyenne, and Dhani were Dawn's human friends and were a Pack in their own right. The fact that Aimee was no longer human changed things, and everyone would need to be let in on exactly what that meant. It was safer for them all if they knew the facts.

Before he could once again slide too far into his thoughts, Kameron stood next to him, frowning. "Are we just soaking in the sun before we head to Gideon's? You know we have dinner in like four minutes so we can be ready for the Pack meeting, right? Get a move on."

He didn't say it unkindly, but Kameron's wolf helped Walker get his head out of his ass where he wanted to stop and growl at anyone who looked at Aimee funny.

"I'm fine, Walker," Aimee whispered, her voice so low that he wasn't sure that even Kameron could hear. "Just breathe, okay? No one is going to get me while I'm standing by you—and now Kameron." She scrunched up her nose. "And, eventually, I suppose you'll teach me to take care of myself as well, right? Because that would be amazing. Just saying."

Once again, she smiled, her way of calming him even as she leaned into him. He wasn't sure what kind of shifter she'd be on the dominance scale, but he had a feeling, either way, she'd be the kind that needed to take care of those around her for her to feel like she was doing something important. That was the type of shifter—wolf or cat—that anyone would be proud of. And he hoped the others saw that when they eventually realized what kind of shifter she was—in all aspects.

He kissed the tip of her nose because he'd found that he loved the way she scrunched it up, then took her hand once again and headed toward Gideon's with Kameron walking behind them.

Soon, they were once again sitting in Gideon's home,

this time around his large dining room table that one of the other wolves in the Pack had made Gideon and Brie as a mating present. It had come with spaces for extra leaves as the family grew, and they'd still almost run out of room just with the immediate family—and that was without children included. The next generation of Brentwoods was still in diapers with more probably on the way as the years passed, but one day, they'd be grown and ready to join them at the table.

The Pack just needed to make sure they stayed alive and well until then. Hence one thing they were here to talk about: the attack on Parker and what to do about Blade and the Aspens. And since Audrey had put herself at risk to save Aimee, it was all interconnected—and worrisome to say the least.

"We've been tracking a few of their sentries to try and see if we can figure out what the fire witch was doing, but they're on complete lockdown right now," Kameron said after he swallowed a mouthful of potatoes. "Audrey's email said the witch is named Scarlett, and that she's the only fire witch with that kind of power near them. And the only one at all within their Pack. She's mated to another cat shifter—though Audrey didn't specify which kind. So the fire witch could have had decades to hone her craft since her life is tied to that of her mate rather than her normal lifespan."

Leah rested against Ryder, a frown on her face. As a water witch, she would have had the lifespan of a human, but when she mated Ryder, she became tied to him. When he died, she would also in most cases, but as they were learning, the way bonds worked these days had changed, and no one knew if that would be the case in the future. The moon goddess's plans were in flux, and they were all forced to wait to see how it settled even as they worked to save their own futures.

Walker leaned forward while Aimee gripped his hand. "You've gotten ahold of Audrey then?" He'd been so focused on getting Aimee healthy after breaking her curse and her change into a shifter that he hadn't been in the loop when it came to the major thing going on within his Pack.

While his attention had been on his mate—and Parker's full recovery—the others had been on the hunt.

Kameron sighed. "Okay, this is what we have. We're not going to the whole Pack with every detail. While they need to know the danger, unless we actually have a plan that uses all of us to take down Blade without harming the innocents within the Aspens, it just leads to too many mistakes and possible stresses that will hurt us more in the end."

Gideon continued for Kameron, a frown on his face and

his wolf in his eyes. The two of them worked together against outside forces when it came to the Pack, but everyone within the hierarchy and in the Brentwood family worked as one. "Blade is trying to attack our Pack subtly, something we didn't have full proof of but we were still pretty certain. There is only one Alpha near us that has that kind of power and hates what we are doing within our Pack. The Aspen Alpha has been dissatisfied—for lack of a better word—with how the Talons and the Redwoods dealt with the Unveiling."

It wasn't as if the Pack had been able to keep the humans from discovering that shifters were real. There had been an all-out battle, with some changing into their animals on camera. They hadn't been able to hide who they were anymore. The government sure has hell hadn't been able to conceal them since many in key places already knew. The resulting war had hurt the Talons, but they had been at peace for over a year now.

Kameron continued. "It still doesn't feel like long enough, though. This peace. And, frankly, we haven't had it since before the Centrals came into being."

Walker held Aimee's hand as he listened to his brothers explain to him what he already knew, but he didn't say anything. Every single one of them needed to be on the same page, and because he'd been so focused on mating bonds and Healing, he'd been left out of some of the other decisions. It was how the Pack worked, but he didn't want to be the weak link.

Blade hadn't been happy when Dawn's former Pack was blessed by the moon goddess and allowed to *officially* become a Pack. Her brother, Cole, had become the Alpha and now joined in on meetings with Gideon and Kade, the Redwood Alpha, to discuss who was sending rogue wolves to the Talon den and, now, using magic to burn them one by one. Scarlett, the fire witch, had even killed one of Dawn's friends from the Centrals, as well as kidnapped Dawn and tried to make her fate a lesson for others. If Dawn were dead, she would only be the beginning unless they learned what Blade wanted and what reprimand he thought they deserved.

"So now the bastard is trying to take out Parker," Mitchell bit out. "Which makes sense in a sick way."

"Why?" Aimee asked, then hid behind Walker's arm as everyone turned to her. "I'm sorry, I didn't mean to speak out of turn."

Gideon shook his head. "No, ask questions, it's why you're all here. And you're Pack, Aimee. You're *supposed* to ask questions. We kind of jumped into this discussion today because that's all we've been talking about, but later at the full Pack meeting, we'll welcome you in and make sure you feel that, okay?"

Brie gave them an apologetic glance. She sat by her

mate and had been taking notes the entire time though Walker was pretty sure she knew as much as Gideon did at this point—probably more since she was one of the smartest people he knew. "I'm sorry we're pushing all of this at you all at once but, apparently, when we mate into the Pack, we hit the ground running."

Those who had been mated in—every single female family member in the room since Brynn wasn't there—gave a soft, nervous laugh. Walker met Kameron's gaze, then Max's, who shrugged. They were the only two unmated wolves left in the family, and he had no idea what they thought about that.

"It's okay," Aimee said. "Walker's been trying to teach me things, but it's a lot."

"And then there's the whole shifter thing," Avery said wryly. She'd been changed against her will at the end of the war with the humans and knew full well what it meant to be a new shifter in a Pack that had been around for ages. Though she wasn't a cat, she'd been able to help Aimee adjust, and Walker was counting on that going forward. Hell, he was relying on a lot of his family.

"Yeah, not to mention the whole cat thing," his mate agreed, and he squeezed her hand.

Gideon gave him a wary look, and Walker held back a growl. There was something going on that he didn't understand, but he'd get to the bottom of it. "But back to your question, Aimee. Parker is the Voice of the Wolves and has met every single Alpha in the country, as well as many in Europe. Parker is a symbol to the other Packs. He always has been with his lineage and position. He'd be even more so if the attack had ended the way Blade wanted it to."

The man in question let out a growl. "Walker Healed me, but it was a close call. What good would my death do Blade?"

Both Brandon and Avery, Parker's mates, growled low at that, and Parker leaned into one, then the other.

"If you're gone, maybe Blade can step in?" Kameron asked, then shook his head. "Not that he'd be the Voice since the moon goddess gave you that job, and he's already an Alpha, but maybe..."

"Maybe he wants to be the *one true* Alpha or something as equally disturbing as that," Walker finished for him, and the rest nodded.

"So, if Parker is out, then that cuts the connection to the other Packs," Aimee said slowly. "At least symbolically."

"Right," Gideon said, his wolf once again in his gaze. "And since we're all learning to live in this new world alongside humans, that connection is beyond important. I don't know what Blade's end game is, and yeah, we haven't *proven* it's him, but something's coming."

They talked a bit more and tried to gather as much information as possible, but the problem was, they didn't *have* that much information. If someone hadn't pieced together every attack made over the past few months, it would have just seemed as if rogues and witches had mounted random attacks against them. But if they were connected, there was something far greater at play.

What, Walker wasn't sure, but he knew his family and Pack would figure it out. They had to.

They ended the family meeting and planned when the full Pack meeting would be, and Walker found himself walking next to his Alpha.

"Be careful," Gideon whispered on their way out of the house.

"What?" Walker asked, his gaze on Aimee as she walked alongside Avery. "What aren't you saying?"

"The Pack is just getting used to her scent, Soon, they'll know *exactly* what she is, even if we don't know the *hows* of it yet, or know what it will mean in terms of her strength and abilities. We're all on a steep learning curve here, and you know some of the old Pack members are resistant to change."

Walker stopped where he was, aware that some of the family was looking at them, but he kept his attention on his Alpha. "Is there a problem that I need to know about?"

Gideon crossed his arms over his massive chest,

looking like the Alpha he was. "I don't know yet, but there's been some rumblings according to Ryder and Mitchell, and since their bonds and duties bring them closest to the Pack when it comes to tiny shifts and changes, I tend to take what they say seriously."

Walker growled, and his brother let out a sigh.

"I don't know, Walker. She's new. She was changed *after* the government made those proclamations. And she's your mate, so we're covered if they find out she's now a shifter instead of a human. Hell, even if they hadn't said mates were allowed, it would have been covered. You know we Alphas won't let that not-quite-a-law stand for much longer, no matter how much pull those in government have."

"But it's the fact that she's a cat that's the real issue," Walker bit out.

Gideon nodded. "They're going to find out and, frankly, we can't keep it from the Pack. We *shouldn't*. That's how distrust between the Alphas and among the rest of the family turns into chaos. But there's been so much change recently that this might be the final tipping point. Hell, I was as shocked as you when Audrey changed, and now we have a lion shifter within our den. I know nothing about how cat shifters operate, and now we have one connected to us through the Pack bonds. I already changed the way the bonds worked when I added

Shane into the Pack to save his life, and now we have this."

Shane was a former human soldier who had been forced into changing not only with a bite but also with a human drug that hadn't quite worked. He'd saved many of their Pack along the way, but his science-based change instead of the usual magic-based one had altered the Pack —and mating—bonds forever. Hence why Walker was so focused on figuring out how to change mating bonds *back* to how they were, or at least learning how to function properly with the current ones. He knew others were missing out on their futures because of how the bonds were now, and Walker wanted to change that, but along the way, he also had to protect his mate in this new life of hers. No wonder he was so behind on what was going on with Blade and the Aspens. Shane was now a Talon wolf, mated to two former Redwood wolves, and guarded the Alpha on most days.

Gideon ran a hand over his face, and Walker saw Brie walk toward them with Aimee by her side, worry evident on both of their faces. "Aimee is a Talon now, and she's yours. The Pack will figure how what to do, and we'll find a way for Aimee to know who she is and how she can fit into the Pack. She can't go back to her old life, Walker. At least, not right now. She's already different than she was, and the humans around her might figure that out."

Walker bit off a curse but nodded. "Yeah, we figured that out already. She still has her family, though."

"And if you can trust them, they can know, but since she's already unemployed in the human world, find her a place within the den until things settle down. The others will learn to live in this new world where there are things other than wolves. Hell, we're learning, too. I know it's a lot, but we've got this. Just one step at a time, right?"

Walker nodded and then held out his arm as Aimee made her way to his side. He held her close, and Gideon did the same with Brie. He vowed to himself that they would figure it all out, but hell if he knew what the next step was.

He knew they were on the verge of something significant. A decision that would change the way their Pack functioned. He just prayed to the moon goddess that his mate finally had time to heal and *be*. Because if not, well, he wasn't sure either of them would survive what was coming.

CHAPTER 14

AIMEE SUCKED in a breath and kept her eyes glued to the very, *very* naked chest in front of her. The pecs she recognized as hers among the vast number of unclad torsos.

She didn't know why the Brentwood brothers and cousins enjoyed playing football with their shirts off to blow off steam after a hard day, but she was truly grateful that she'd been invited to sit and watch. While many of Pack had joined in, there were more spectators than she'd expected.

And, at least in her opinion, the sexiest one on the field was *hers*. She wasn't sure whether this irrational jealousy she felt when some of the single women in the seating areas around the field stared or gave Walker hungry looks was because he was *hers,* or because she had this new cat inside her fighting for control.

Either way, she wasn't sure she enjoyed having to hold herself back from knocking into some of the women panting after her mate. It was a new feeling, this irrational need for her to mark and claim him as her own.

It had been six days since she was changed.

Six days since he'd stripped the curse from her soul, and gave her a new chance at life.

And in those six days, they hadn't truly touched.

They'd talked, learned, researched mating bonds and large tomes of text to see if there was any hint about what kind of shifter she was and what she could expect. They'd slept next to each other in his bed every night, and she had relished how he held her close. She'd understood that she'd be forced to stay within the den for a while until she figured out how to live this new life and not let the outside world know what she was now, but that was fine by her. She didn't have much left for her beyond her friends outside of the den anyway, and it wasn't as if she were truly close to her family. They hadn't called her once, and she knew they probably wouldn't unless they needed something. It was how they worked, and how she was used to living.

But even with all of that talking, Walker had pulled away from her. Maybe at first, it was because he'd been worried that he was hurting her so soon after everything that happened, but she was fully healed now and had more energy than she'd ever had in her life. She'd even filled out in the past few days, surprising the hell out of her one morning when she studied herself in the mirror. Her curves had rounded just enough that it was noticeable that she wasn't on death's door any longer. Even her breasts were firmer and just a bit larger as they overfilled her bra.

And yet, Walker hadn't touched her.

Now, she was worried that they'd moved too fast, and he now thought he'd made a mistake. Maybe he'd only taken her as his mate to save her life or because he wanted to see if he could fix the mating bonds like he'd been trying to do before he even met her. She hated this self-doubt because it was starting to consume her. So much so that she was worried she wouldn't be able to find her place in the Pack.

It wasn't as if they needed a waitress, after all.

For now, she was helping Walker at the clinic, but with Leah on staff, she didn't know if he truly needed her or if it was just something she could do with her time.

She knew she needed to figure it out though and stop analyzing every single move Walker made. It was making her crazy, and she wouldn't be able to thrive in this new life if she was constantly afraid that everyone thought they'd made a mistake by rescuing her.

Someone elbowed her, and she glanced over at Dhani, who had taken the spot next to her. She and Cheyenne had shown up that day to spend the afternoon watching hot, sweaty men play football, and then later, have dinner at Dawn's. They knew what Aimee was now, but that didn't mean anyone *truly* understood what that meant.

"Stop frowning," Dhani said softly, though Aimee could hear her clearly. She hadn't adjusted to her new senses yet, and Walker warned her that they would get even stronger after her first shift.

As the full moon was still a week or so away, she had time to worry about that, as well. It was, apparently, what she did now.

"Am I frowning?" Aimee asked, her gaze on Walker as he bent forward for the snap. His jeans rode low, and she was pretty sure her mouth watered at the sight.

"Yeah, you are, and I have no idea why. You're healthy —praise everything for that—you have a *very* sexy man you get to sleep with running around shirtless and sweaty in front of you, and you're surrounded by people who care about you. What's wrong? Do you need some chocolate or something to perk you up?"

Cheyenne leaned around Dhani. "Did someone say chocolate?"

"I have chocolate," Dawn said from Aimee's other side. She handed over a bag of chocolate caramels, and each of the girls took one.

Aimee moaned when she took a bite, and Walker's head turned sharply in her direction at the sound. She blushed and waved the half-eaten chocolate at him, and he smiled. That grin did something warm to her insides, and she tried not to make too much of a scene when surrounded by so many people she didn't know. The Pack hadn't exactly warmed up to her yet—hence why her friends surrounded her, rather than some of the other wolves she didn't know. Walker's family sat next to them, as well. and did their best to show that Aimee was one of theirs, but it was still awkward as hell because so many of the others didn't know what to do with a cat shifter in their midst.

They didn't know where she would land in the hierarchy, nor did they know anything else about how she would shift or hunt or even use magic. Because, apparently, some of the wolves each held special...powers, but Aimee was pretty sure that wouldn't be her. She was already the odd woman out because she was a lion—something she was never going to get used to thinking—and she didn't want anything else to single her out in a Pack that had already been through so much.

Before she could say anything else to her friends,

however, Walker prowled toward her, his gaze intent. She looked up at him as he hovered over her before he knelt in front of her, wrapped his hand around the back of her head, and brought her face to his for a deep kiss.

This time, her moan was something else entirely, and she didn't care that others were around her, watching, listening, probably talking and murmuring.

"Dhani told you to stop frowning, and I agree," he said quietly against her lips, though she knew at least Dawn would have heard him. "When we get home later, we'll talk about what I felt along our bond."

Her brows rose. "What did you feel?" She only felt warmth along her side usually, and she wasn't sure what else would happen with it. She'd heard that some mates could talk to each other along it; others could feel where each other were no matter where they stood. For now, she just knew that Walker was *there*, nothing else.

"We'll talk about it later." He kissed her again. "Got a game to finish." He grinned then, and she couldn't help but fall that much more for him. "And the fact that we can feel the mating bonds? Hell, Aimee, something is different with them. Something..."

"Normal," Brandon said from behind Walker. She hadn't noticed the other man walk up, but then again, her attention had been solely on her mate and his incredible lips. "They feel like they should. I've been noticing it for the past couple of days, but it's taken a while for me to figure out exactly what it means. Ever since you mated in, Aimee, something's different. A *good* different."

Aimee was about to say something, though she wasn't sure what since that statement had come out of nowhere, but before she could, someone gasped on the field.

Brandon and Walker turned, and Aimee stood, putting her hand on Walker's back for support since he was so close to her, she didn't want them to topple over.

On the field, a man in jeans and a t-shirt stood in front of one shirtless man, each staring at the other with wide eyes. Aimee recognized the one in the shirt as one of the sentries who had let her into the den a few times before she was Pack. Since he'd come from the direction of one of the gates, he must have just gotten off shift.

The two men stared at each other as if neither had seen the other before, yet she knew they had to know each other since they worked together within the den.

"Holy shit," Cheyenne whispered when the two men cupped each other's faces and kissed as if there were no tomorrow.

"Uh, does this happen often, because making out on the field while playing football might be something I want to join in on," Dhani put in, making everyone around her chuckle.

Brandon rubbed his hand over his chest, and his two

mates came up to him, holding him close. "They're mates," the Omega said after a moment. "I mean, they aren't bonded yet, but they just figured out that they're mates."

Aimee looked up at Walker, confused. "It can happen that quickly?"

The two men went off toward, presumably, one of their houses for some privacy, as Walker answered. "Not usually. Well, it hasn't been like that for a while anyway. And even then, Adam and Ben have known each other for years, so their wolves should have recognized one another long before this. Yet with the mating bonds having been out of tune for so long, things got a little cloudy."

"So maybe the bonds are coming back or something?" Dhani said, a frown on her face. She looked over her shoulder and stiffened, but when Aimee looked to where her friend's gaze had landed, she only saw the rest of the Brentwoods, nothing that would have made Dhani frown.

"This is good," Walker said, awe in his voice. "This is really good. Though I wish I knew the *why* of it."

Aimee wrapped her arms around his middle, and he lifted his arm to hold her tightly. "You'll figure it out. But progress is good, right? And you have another mating to celebrate, from what I can tell."

Walker smiled again, and the others came over to hug and laugh with them.

"It seems we might need to have a huge mating ceremony soon for a few couples," Gideon said. "After all, the two of you still need to have yours under the moon."

Walker kissed the top of her head, and that new warmth inside her—her cat—purred. "Sounds good to me."

"We going to finish the game?" Kameron asked, his voice a little cold. He was always cold around her, though she didn't know why. There was just something about Kameron that made her feel like she was missing something, but she could never quite figure out what it was.

"Oh, yes, because playing football is what you should do to celebrate," Dhani said sarcastically, and Kameron just glared.

Aimee tugged on her friend's arm. "Hey, what's wrong?"

Dhani shrugged and turned her attention away from the glaring wolf. "Nothing."

Aimee didn't quite believe her and was thankful when the others went back to their game, this time with a little more lightness to their steps. Walker even patted her on the butt as he walked away, and she couldn't help but stare.

Maybe she was wrong that he didn't want her. Maybe she just needed to breathe.

The others resumed their game, and she sat next to

her friends, aware that others were staring, but she wasn't sure if it was because of the Brentwoods or her. She clenched her fists, her fingertips burning. Walker had warned her that she'd have to get used to this new side of herself, but because she hadn't shifted yet, she wasn't sure what would come of it all.

Something pricked her senses, and she looked over her shoulder, trying to see what it was. She frowned and swore she had heard someone call out, but no one else seemingly had. Maybe she was losing her mind even without the curse to aid her in doing that. She was just about to turn back to the game when she heard another shout.

Once again, no one else turned around.

Worried now, with her cat rising to the surface—though she wasn't sure if that was the right way to say it or even understand the feeling—she stood up, ignoring her friends' worried looks.

Another call—this time, a scream.

She ran toward it without a second glance, not caring that others were calling out to her or that Walker was running behind her. She *knew* it wasn't a trick, *knew* she wasn't the one in danger. It was something else.

Aimee jumped over a fallen log and ran through the surrounding forest until she came up to a ravine, the edge jagged from where a mudslide had taken out part of the walkway at least a few weeks ago.

This time, the shout that came was louder.

A cry from a child *down* in the ravine.

Letting her instincts take over, she scaled down the wall, her claws poking through her fingertips so she could steady herself. It burned, and she had no idea how she'd done it, but she told herself if she thought too hard about what was happening, she'd fall or end up hurting the child.

A little girl of about five or six lay on one of the jagged rocks, just below the sightline of anyone who might look down over the edge of the cliff. She had a bloody knee and dirt on her face, but otherwise, she seemed all right. She must have rolled down the side yet, somehow, hadn't fallen any farther.

Tearstains made tracks in the dirt on her face, and Aimee held back tears of her own.

"Aimee!" Walker called out.

"I'm down here!" She knelt in front of the little girl, careful not to lean any way too much or she'd overbalance and fall. "What's your name, honey?"

"Hannah," the girl whispered. "I'm not supposed to be out of daycare. I'm in trouble."

Aimee held out her hand, but the little girl stayed where she was. "No, you aren't. Not right this second.

Can you help me get you back up? I'm sure your mommy and daddy miss you."

Hannah shrunk into herself.

"Walker?" she called out.

"We're coming, baby. I can hear you and Hannah. I just need to get a few ropes, and Max is on his way with them."

"Ropes?" she called back, doing her best not to sound panicked.

"I'm a wolf, baby. Apparently, cats climb better than wolves." There wasn't panic in his voice, but something told her that while he found that interesting, he was still freaking out for her. And now that she thought about what exactly she'd done, she was freaking out, too.

The rock below her and Hannah shifted suddenly, and she sucked in a breath. No panicking, not in front of the little girl who was relying on her. "Hannah? Can you climb onto my back?"

Hannah wasn't that big, and though Aimee was pretty short, she had her new shifter strength to get her through. At least she hoped she did because if she was wrong, they were both in trouble.

The rock moved again, and Hannah leapt toward her. It took her new reflexes for Aimee to catch her, and soon, the little girl was on Aimee's back, and the two of them were shaking.

"Aimee? Hold on, baby. We're coming."

Walker was calling her *baby* with others around. He must really be freaking scared. Frankly, so was she—not that she could show that fear, since she had to be strong for this little girl that she had heard from so far away. She'd think about the *how* of that later.

"I think I need to climb up now," she said quickly, doing her best to keep the fear out of her voice. The rock moved again, and she sucked in a breath. She dug her claws into the rock and dirt in front of her and prayed.

"Shit," Walker whispered, then cleared his throat. "Okay, Aimee. Be *really* careful. I'll pull you up as soon as I can reach you." Others talked around them, but she only focused on Walker. If she didn't, she'd start hyperventilating since what she was doing was so far out of her sphere of normal it wasn't funny.

"Hold on tight," Aimee said as calmly as she could.

Hannah's hold tightened and, thankfully, she didn't cut off Aimee's air, though it was close with how hard the little girl clung to her neck. Then, focusing only on what was in front of her, Aimee started climbing. Her hands burned, and her shoulders ached, but she kept going. She'd gone farther down the rock wall than she realized, but there was no going back now. As soon as her feet were off the ledge below, it crumbled away, forcing a whimper out of Hannah's throat. It was that sound that allowed Aimee to keep her own gasp in.

When she got halfway up, the wall curved slightly, and she was able to see Walker. He was holding the edge of the rock face with one hand, others around him either holding him up or doing the same. As soon as she saw him, she almost let out a relieved breath but knew if she didn't keep going, she'd make a mistake.

Again, she let instinct take over, and in five more climbs, she was able to reach Walker. He bent forward and gripped her hard, and tears stung her eyes.

Kameron was on his other side and plucked Hannah from her back, and Aimee clung to Walker as he hoisted them both up. Things moved quickly then as two people who had to be Hannah's parents, as well as a woman who Aimee remembered was the head of the daycare came rushing forward. Walker held Aimee close, kissed her hard, then went to see if Hannah needed any medical help.

While everyone moved around her, trying to shore up the edge of the ravine so this accident wouldn't happen again, as well as figure out *how* Hannah had fallen where no one had heard her, Aimee stood there, dazed and a little lost.

She'd saved someone's life.

How...how had she done that? And as the reality of

what she'd just done settled around her, Walker's arms held her close.

"Hannah will be fine. Just a few cuts and bruises I already Healed. Now, let me get a good look at you."

She held out her hands, but they were uncut, and her claws had long since disappeared. She wasn't sure she could call them back if she tried since she had no idea how they had shown up to begin with. She had no clue how *any* of that had just happened.

Hannah and her parents came up next to hug her close and say their thanks, and it was all Aimee could do not to break down into tears and wonder how the hell her life had come to this. Others in the Pack hugged her, as well, even those who, just an hour ago, had given her curious and almost distrustful looks. It seemed saving a child's life changed things. To what, she didn't know, but she did know that this was a *moment*. One she'd relive forever, wondering how the hell she'd done it at all.

Walker kissed the top of her head and glared at those who hadn't been quite as nice to her before, but he didn't say anything. She wasn't sure what there to say anyway. Someone had held her friends back at the field, as no one knew exactly what they would be facing, and she had a feeling there would be hell to pay for that. Of the four of them, Dhani and Cheyenne had always been the fiercest, and they were the only two humans left of the bunch.

When Kameron came up, she was beyond tired and just wanted to go back to Walker's house—her home now she supposed—to talk about what had happened. Only, it seemed as if she weren't going to get that option at the moment.

"You heard her call out, didn't you? From all the way by the field." Kameron studied her so intently, she felt as though she were under a microscope.

"Yes..." She frowned. "But why could I do that when no one else could?"

Walker squeezed her before speaking. "It could either be because you're a lion shifter and that's how your senses work, or...or it's a power of some sort that you'll grow into."

She turned toward her mate, her eyes wide. "A power?"

"Like those with sensory memory or healing that isn't like what I have."

"From what I can tell, your reflexes are super sharp, and your senses even more so." He tilted his head as if he were in his wolf form. "That could be good for protection within the den walls. Perhaps, one day, you'll be one of my soldiers. Interesting."

Walker let out a growl. "She's still mine."

Aimee just stared between the two of them, confused. A soldier? That hadn't once crossed her mind. She'd been a waitress with no money, not a fighter. And yet she hadn't hesitated to save Hannah and run headlong into danger.

She didn't know what any of that might mean in the long run, but as she stood in Walker's arms, she didn't feel like a lost human with a disease she couldn't cure any longer. She might not know who she was, but she wasn't weak.

Her mate kissed the top of her head, and she let out a breath, knowing that she belonged.

Finally.

KAMERON

IT WASN'T SUPPOSED to happen to him. That much Kameron knew. Of all his siblings, he was the one who hated change the most. While the others leaned into their histories as fate unfolded, he'd been the cold one, the steadfast one who was forced to search in all directions for what could happen if their destinies altered the very fabric and safety of their lives.

His brother, Walker, had been so focused on how to fix what was wrong with the mating bonds that he hadn't thought of what would happen when suddenly, a wolf could feel what could be his after being numb to it for so long.

As the others around him went over how Aimee could have possibly heard the little girl from so far away and went into detail talking about her abilities, Kameron only had eyes for one woman as she made her way toward them.

Dhanielle, Dhani for short, pushed past grown wolves who were far taller and stronger than she was, with Cheyenne right on her tail as they made their way to Aimee.

"Next time you decide to play hero and run away from us, don't leave us with a bunch of wolves who won't let us go anywhere," Dhani snapped before hugging her friend close. There were tears in her eyes even as there was anger and worry in her tone. He'd never known such a difficult woman, and he wasn't sure he wanted to get to know her more.

Of course, if his wolf had anything to say about it, he wouldn't have a choice.

Gideon came up to him then and whispered in his ear. "One of the scouts just got back. We need to talk about Blade."

Kameron nodded, his attention still on Dhani, though he didn't want it to be. What he needed to focus on was the Alpha of the Aspens. He *needed* to know why the wolf had a stick up his ass when it came to the Talons and why he was gunning for Parker and the rest of them so hard. He didn't think it was a coincidence that so many attacks had come in the past year even if they seemed unconnected. He didn't believe in coincidences. It was his duty to protect the Pack from outside forces, and he would stop at nothing to make that happen—even if that meant focusing only on what came at them rather than who could be in front of him.

He pulled his gaze from Dhani as she turned to him and faced Gideon instead. He needed to protect his Alpha, his people, his den. He didn't have time to look at a woman who could change everything.

Because Walker had been right. Brandon had been right. What they'd seen on the field as Adam and Ben found each other and realized they were mates had been an omen.

The mating bonds were coming back in full force.

And Kameron's wolf knew who could be his.

But he had no idea what the hell he was going to do about it.

DHANI

A WOMAN STOOD in front of her, her long, white gown billowing in the breeze. Dhani didn't recognize her, but there was something just familiar enough that it intrigued her. She didn't know where she was either. It seemed as if she stood in the middle of a dark cavern with no other lights except the ones that illuminated the woman in front of her, but she had no idea how she'd gotten there or *why* she was there at all.

The woman stared at her, her eyes a pale gray that seemed to shine without any light making them do so.

"Your time is almost here," the woman said, her voice taking on an airy quality that made her sound as if she were all around Dhani instead of just in front of her.

"What are you talking about?"

"You will have to be strong, Dhanielle. Stronger than

you know. But the dreams do not lie. The time has come. When the last star falls, and the connection burns, you will find your place among them, and all that has been forgotten will be revealed."

And with that, the woman threw her head back and screamed, smoke and white flames enveloping her as she faded away, leaving Dhani standing alone, shaking.

"What...what was that?"

And before anyone—*anything*—could answer her, Dhani woke up in her bed, drenched with sweat yet shaking with cold. Her sheets were a tangled mess around her legs, and her hands shook as she swiped at her wet hair that clung to her face.

Had it all been a dream?

It hadn't felt like a dream at the time, and even as she sat in her bed, her heart racing as if she'd run a mile at full sprint, she wasn't sure she could quite believe it hadn't been real.

"It was just a nightmare," she whispered to herself, her voice sounding loud in the quiet room void of all other sounds. "Just a dream."

But even as she tried to settle back to sleep, she worried that it had been something more. Something dangerous. Her body fell into rest as the last worries slid through her mind, making her wonder what could be coming, and perhaps, what was already here.

CHAPTER 15

WALKER HAD no idea why he was nervous, but then again, he'd never cooked a full meal with his mate so they could have their date inside their house and act like a normal couple instead of mythically connected shifters who seemed to be surrounded by constant change and threats.

Aimee was back in the bedroom—*their* bedroom—finishing her makeup since they'd wanted to do a full date and not just a random dinner in sweats. Though come to think of it, he enjoyed their meals in sweats followed by cuddling on the couch, but they hadn't had much of that lately, and honestly, had moved so fast into mating that they were going backwards in terms of this dance of theirs. For two shifters who had grown up knowing how mating worked and how the bond would cement their relationship, that wasn't a bad thing. For a human, however, especially one who had been thrust into the paranormal world without her knowledge even before she knew about Dawn's true identity, mating bonds and their lack of true dating and time was an actual issue.

Or at least, he thought it was.

Aimee hadn't complained, but he also wanted to make sure she experienced the human part of what they were, as well—not just the magical pieces. She hadn't asked for any of this but hadn't backed down when their worlds changed.

So, he'd do what he could to make sure she had *everything* she wanted. Or at least, he'd be sure to give her everything that was within his power.

And that included him making her dinner before they watched a movie while sitting on his couch. It wasn't as if they could go out into the real world at this point and date like normal people. First, they were anything but normal, even if he tried to pretend that they were for a few moments. Secondly, they had to hide Aimee's connection to the Pack as long as they could so others wouldn't find how that she'd not only been changed, but into something different than a wolf.

So a night in at home where they didn't talk about Pack issues or what the Aspen Pack might be planning would have to suffice as a date where they could actually get to know one another better.

Aimee's scent drifted toward him before she entered the room. His wolf perked up as if he'd been taking a nap and was suddenly eager to see who held the delicious scent. When Walker turned to her, she smiled at him, her eyes hesitant, but only for a moment. Then she moved toward him, and he held out an arm.

When she settled against his side, his wolf pressed into him, wanting more contact. And as much as Walker wanted nothing more than to strip his mate down and have his way with her, he knew she needed time to adjust to this new part of her. She'd almost died in his arms, and him fucking her hard against the counter like he wanted to didn't reflect the calm and cool Walker he tried so hard to be.

"So, what are we making again?" She peered around him and looked at the wok on the stove.

He let out a curse, then turned back to the meal, using the wooden spoon to scrape the veggies and chicken off the bottom of the pan before they burned.

"Stir-fry. Not *good* stir-fry, mind you. You'd think after all these years on this planet I'd find a way to be a better cook, but sadly, I'm a failure."

Aimee's eyes danced, and she took the other spoon to

fluff the rice he'd already cooked but had on a warmer. "I'll help you learn if you want."

He froze for a moment, then leaned down to kiss the back of her neck. "Oh, yeah? I think I like that." What he *really* liked was the fact that she was talking about something long-term in their future. They'd gone about their relationship in an unusual way, but they were finding their path.

Together, they finished dinner, then took their plates to the table where they sat side by side next to candles and talked about nothing and everything. There was no talk of wars, curses, or battles taking place when it was just the two of them. He knew things would be different soon, and in the morning they'd have to go back to the real world, but for this night, they could pretend and just...*be*.

"So, you're really a reincarnated wolf, just like your brothers?" Aimee asked, her nose scrunched. "I mean... how on earth did you find that out, and what does it even mean?"

He snorted, shaking his head before taking a sip of his drink. "Brandon figured it out when he was in the middle of his mating heat with Parker and Avery. Apparently, while Parker is a descendent of the first hunter, the three of us, Brandon, Kameron and I, are the reincarnated souls of the first three the hunter made into wolves."

Aimee's eyes grew round, and Walker couldn't help but laugh.

"I know, I know. It sounds crazy."

"I was cursed by a witch we haven't been able to find and am now a shifter mated to another shifter who isn't going to be the same animal as I am. I think we passed crazy long ago."

"True enough. So, as for what all this means, the best we can figure out, is that it connects us to our wolves more. It helped Brandon, like I said before, when it came to the wards, which were failing after years of neglect, but the idea that my soul was already on this earth once hasn't really affected me much. I don't know about Kameron, though." And knowing how tight-lipped his brother was about anything personal, he wasn't sure his triplet even cared.

"That's...okay, that's something to get used to." Aimee said after a moment. They'd cleared their plates and were now sitting on the couch in the living room, pressed tightly into one another and just...talking. He liked it and hated the fact that they didn't have a lot of time for nights like this anymore. "What did you mean about neglect before?" she asked, her voice low as if she knew it was a difficult subject.

And hell, it was, but she needed to know everything.

It was a large part of their Pack's history, and she needed to know everything.

"The Alpha before Gideon was our father. He...well, let's just say he was a sadistic bastard who made Blade look like a puppy." When she slid her hand into his, he was able to continue. Their mating bond pulsed, and he could breathe. "He became insular and refused to let the Talons help any other Pack or even become their allies. We didn't connect with the Redwoods until much later." He paused. "Until it was almost too late for them, actually."

That had been a long war for the Redwoods, one they all remembered vividly even though it had been over thirty years. He'd tell her that story soon so she could know it all.

"The moon goddess even turned away from us. My father...well, he not only beat us down physically and emotionally, he destroyed anyone that went against him and thought they could try to save our Pack." He swallowed hard. "He killed our mother, his mate. Or had her killed. I don't really know. Only Gideon does, and he refuses to tell us. Frankly, I don't think any of us have actually asked."

"Oh, Walker." She climbed into his lap, and he held her close. "I'm so sorry."

He kissed the top of her head, his wolf settling down

to rest at her touch. "My uncles, the former hierarchy, were just as bad. The one uncle we thought was on our side ended up being the worst." It had been Leo who revealed them to the humans when they thought all was lost. He'd had so many killed for his own greed, yet there was nothing they could do. The wolf was long dead, dust in the wind.

"When Gideon was able to fight back, somehow, we all found the strength to help. The old guard was gone, our family broken, yet the new generation rose up and tried to make our Pack better. It's taken years, but we're finally at a place where we are strong."

He was trying to say they could protect her.

"I'm only sad that he's gone so I can't kill him for you," Aimee growled then froze, her eyes going wide. "Whoa."

He kissed the tip of her nose, aware that her cat was now out to play, even though she was still learning control. "Your cat is bloodthirsty. I like it."

"It's weird."

He kissed her again and held her close. "We're pretty weird ourselves, so that works." When he let out a sigh, she snuggled in close. "That's not the best conversation to have for date night, is it?"

"We're learning more about each other," she whispered. "It seems like the perfect conversation."

And as they continued, he settled onto the couch,

relaxing for the first time in ages. He had his mate, his future, the one woman he was connected to in all the world.

He was falling in love with her, or really, had already done so, but he'd wait to tell her until they were both ready. It was all just a little too much, too soon, but when the time came, he'd tell her his soul, his heart. And hope she felt the same. In the end, if anyone tried to destroy what they had, he'd end them.

Healer or no.

ULTIMATUM

PLANS SHOULD BE KEPT and then made better as things got in the way. Blade was sure there were other sayings out there that probably made sense, but he didn't care right then. He was pissed and had to deal with Pack bullshit before he went about fixing everything that hadn't turned out the way it should have.

His wolves needed time with their Alpha, and he was nothing if not a benevolent leader. But they were now starting to worry that they hadn't seen their Beta in a while. Not that Blade actually gave a flying fuck since it was his Beta's fault that they were in some of this position to begin with.

Audrey had betrayed them, and that would *not* be tolerated.

And if the others in the Pack didn't start backing

down from questioning him about Audrey, he was going to share with them that she had betrayed them all by telling the Talons about the existence of *others* within the Pack. He'd saved them by keeping all of that a secret as he knew other wolves would want to eradicate them once they knew—and he made sure he told his people that often. But he'd *felt* it through the Pack bonds when Audrey changed another into a lion. Oh, the newly changed might not have ended up in his Pack, but Audrey had smelled of Talon far too often lately for his liking, so he had put two and two together.

She would pay for what she'd done, and pay for it slowly. Day by day until she regretted ever defying her Alpha and putting him in a position where he was forced to punish her. It was her fault that she was hurting, her fault he'd been forced to torture her.

Her fault.

Always.

"You're growling again," Scarlett whined from her perch on one of the stools in his office. "What are you thinking about this time? Audrey? Or that damn wolf who won't die?" She was the one to growl this time, even if she wasn't a shifter.

"Fucking Parker," he spat. "How did he survive your spell?"

"Because that damn Healer was too close, that's how."

She slid from the stool and began to pace around his office. "*Walker.*" She said the name like a curse, and Blade agreed with her on that.

"He Healed the wolf, and now they know someone is coming after them. Someone with a fire witch, with your power."

Scarlett turned on him. "Your Beta probably told them, if they hadn't already guessed. And they would have known I was connected to you, or at least what was coming at them anyway from when I killed that other wolf and took the Central wolf who's now mated into the Talons. I've sacrificed a lot for this cause, and I'll be damned if I let some little Healer wolf mess everything up for us."

Blade liked the sound of her anger because it meant she wasn't going to back down and would stay on his side. As much as he hated relying on others, he needed the fire witch to do some of the footwork for him while he stayed in the shadows. His plans were almost ready, and what he'd been working on for decades would come into the light soon. But for now, he would use the witch until there was nothing left. It was what he did.

"Then we'll get rid of Walker." He shrugged as if it meant nothing, but he knew getting at the wolf wouldn't be easy, not with everyone working so hard to try and figure out who was coming for them.

Scarlett's eyes lit up. "I have an idea about that. He just mated that human, or rather, I suppose she's a cat now, isn't she?"

He nodded, his wolf growling. His spies had been able to tell him that much, but he didn't know much about the woman. "We can take her out, too. It would solve the problem of the Talons now having something they shouldn't."

The witch smiled. "And I know how we can make it worth it. I have a...shall we say, friend. Someone who is beyond angry right now because she lost the human. She'll be glad to have her back—in whatever state she can have her."

This time, Blade perked up. "What do you mean? What friend?"

Scarlett waved him off. "An air witch who's been using that family for generations to stay alive or something. I don't know the magic. It's not my kind of curse, and since I'm mated to a shifter, I haven't needed anything like that, but now that, somehow—and I bet it was the Healer—they broke the curse, my friend isn't happy."

"So, call her. We'll use her and make sure Walker and his new mate regret standing in our way."

Scarlett smiled, and he saw flames dance in her eyes. That used to worry him, the amount of power she held, but not anymore. He used her magic for himself, and with the intensity of it, they couldn't lose.

He'd take out the Healer for daring to stand in his path, and the little cat would be cursed again—a fate worse than death if he imagined right. And then he'd take out Parker and finish his plans.

Yes, this would work, and while he waited, he'd pay Audrey a visit.

She hadn't broken yet, after all, and he wanted her screams.

Always.

CHAPTER 16

WALKER WANTED to be anyone but himself just then, but he knew there wasn't another way to get through this. He knelt by his mate as she cried out, her body bending and breaking as she started her first shift. He was a Healer, damn it, but there was nothing he could do to ease her pain and help her shift along. He could only sit back and watch, soothing her cries as she went from human to lion.

The first shift was always the worst when one had been changed from human to shifter instead of being born with the ability, and that wasn't something he could change, even as a Healer. When pups were first able to shift, the moon goddess shielded them from the pain so they could learn the process easier. When they went through puberty, the shield fell away, and they had to learn to shift through the agony, but at least they knew the steps to go from one form to another. When an adult was forced into the change, there were no barriers from the pain, and they had to persevere through it—tears and screams and all.

The next day was the full moon and the hunt, but since the moon was already so full now, he and Aimee had decided that she would try to shift for the first time tonight. No one in his family had wanted her first shift to be surrounded by so many people, and they had agreed that the two of them could go off alone and try to make this work the first time. Others would be curious, and even though they would try to give her privacy, the thoughts would still be there. It would shed even more of a spotlight on her and make the change about something far greater than her. In a world where she hadn't had much choice, he wanted first shift to be about *her* and not what it all could mean in the grand scheme of things.

Aimee let out another whimper, and he sat next to her face, barely holding back the urge to lift her into his arms and hold her close. Her skin would be far too sensitive right then for him to touch her without causing her more discomfort. He just had to sit next to her and let her know that he was there for her. Once she was in her cat form, he would begin the long shift as well, and then they would run together. That was their plan anyway. At this point, he might just wait for her to shift, then put her on his lap and hold her until the sun rose. He wasn't sure his wolf could do any more, not when their mate was in trouble, and there was nothing they could do about it.

After what seemed like hours but had been less than ten minutes, Aimee let out a chuffing noise, and he blinked at her.

"You are fucking beautiful."

She tilted her head sideways, and he wasn't sure if it was the cat he was talking to or his mate. She was in the in-between stage where the internal battle over dominance would take time—and a few more shifts—to get right. For now, though, all he could do was stare at his mate and know that he was one lucky bastard.

"You know, I *knew* you'd be a lion, but seeing you in the flesh, all gold and silky, it's something else. You're stunning." He grinned and ran a hand down her soft fur. It was shorter than a wolf's and felt just slightly different, but he loved it. She was all sleek and powerful, and he had a feeling she would become a force to be reckoned with once she grew into her new life. Kameron was already on the hunt for her to be on his team, and while Walker enjoyed having her by his side at work, he knew the best place for her would be where she shined. And after he'd seen her hunt like she had in human form to save Hannah, he had a feeling she'd be a soldier soon.

He was just so damn proud of her.

"I'm going to shift now, and then we can go for a run. Want to walk around a bit in the clearing and get used to your new form?" He kissed the top of her head, and she purred. *Purred.* Hell, he had a feeling he was going to love her as a cat. "I won't be long."

She tried to nod, realized that it wasn't an easy movement in animal form, then slowly walked away, each step more careful than the last as she learned to walk on four paws instead of two feet.

He quickly stripped out of his clothes and pulled on his bond to his wolf, his inner beast eager to join their mate on a hunt. The change came far quicker than he'd expected, and he had a feeling it had to do with the fact that neither of his forms wanted to wait. Soon, he was at Aimee's side. He licked her head, then bit down gently on the ruff of her neck. She chuffed, then did the same to him, marking him as hers. Later, they would mark each other once again in human form, claiming one another as mates, though the bond was already there and settling.

He took the lead, keeping an eye out as she ran beside him through the forest. His animal was far more suited to the terrain than hers, but she kept up, the power and grace in her movements breathtaking. She had a decent endurance level from what he could see, and he had a feeling as she grew into her animal, it would be even better. He knew his family would *love* hunting with her when the time came. But for now, she was all his, and he relished the run—and his mate.

When they were through, he led her through to the clearing and began to shift back. Aimee was already a pro at it, though she'd never gone from animal to human before, and he knew she would be as dominant as he was, at least. She might even end up being more dominant in the end, but that didn't bother him in the least. After watching her almost fade away because of a curse, seeing her stronger than him would be a feast for the eyes.

When they were back in human form, naked and sweaty, he pounced on her, needing her taste more than his next gasp of air. She arched under him, her pussy wet and hot as his cock pressed against her.

She tasted of shifter and *his,* and he wanted to pound into her, fucking her hard until they both came, screaming each other's names loudly enough for the entire den to hear that they were both claimed. Both *taken.*

When she pulled back, arching her breasts so her nipples brushed against the hair of his chest, he groaned.

"Thank the goddess," she whispered, echoing what those in the den said of their deity. "I've been waiting for you to touch me like this. I thought you didn't want me. Or at least, were afraid to hurt me."

He growled and bit her lip. "I was giving you space.

Do you not feel my dick hard and ready to be inside you? Of *course,* I wanted you."

She reached between them and gripped his length, giving it a squeeze that left him breathless and aching. "You say that, but you didn't fuck me. Didn't *act* like you wanted me. Not like this."

He kissed her hard then bit her lip again. "You're saying dirty words, I think I like it."

"I'll like it more when you mark me as yours and claim me again *while* you get this," she squeezed, making his eyes cross, "inside me again. I've missed you. It feels like ages since we were together.'

He sighed and rocked his length between her folds, making them both pant. "It has been ages. I thought I was giving you time."

She licked her lips, arching up. "If I wanted time, I would have told you."

He'd made his mate feel as though he hadn't wanted her. He would have to make it up to her. "I'm sorry." He thrust the tip of himself inside her. "I want you." He thrust in and out, just a bit more. "Always. I'll always want you." He slid home, hard, eliciting a gasp of pleasure from her. She rolled them over, surprising him, and seated herself on top of him. The action left her breasts accessible, and he cupped them with his hands, pinching and rolling her nipples. Each time he did, her inner walls clenched around his dick, and he pumped up into her harder.

They made love with abandon, biting and clawing at each other as she rode him, and then he pulled out and flipped her onto her knees so he could fuck her from behind. She thrust back against him, meeting his hips as he slid in deep. Soon, they were both panting and sweaty and closer to coming than they had been before.

Her endurance, apparently, had been increased in more ways than one.

"Touch yourself," he growled into her ear as he hovered over her. "Make yourself come on my dick, then I'm going to lick you clean."

She shivered and did as he ordered, calling his name as she squeezed his cock with her pussy. Then he pulled out of her, slid down between her legs even though his cock ached with the need for release, and latched on to her clit. She was still coming as she rose again, her cunt drenched as she pushed against his face. He fucked her with three fingers, curling his hand, then pulled out and speared her with his cock again as she came once more.

He pumped in and out of her, fast and hard, and she clawed his back before biting his shoulder, marking her as his. He came hard then, and she joined him, her body wrenching away from him as she arched. He bit her nipple, marking her there as well as where he had before, then collapsed on top of her, spent, and in fucking love. He was still inside her, hard and hot as he spoke to her.

"I love you, Aimee mine. Fucking love you. I love your strength, your passion, your fearlessness. I just love you."

He kissed away her tears as she cupped his face and licked his lips. "I love you, too. I think I started falling for you the moment you caught me as I fell through the wards, only I didn't realize it then. I love you so much. I never thought I'd find something like this. Someone like you."

He smiled then, his body relaxing as he held onto her out in the clearing and under the stars. "And the best part is that we have a long while to enjoy that."

She snuggled into him, their bodies still connected. "That sounds...perfect."

Yeah, it did, and he knew that, no matter what, he'd fight to keep it that way. Even if it meant doing things no Healer should do. Because of Aimee, he'd fight, he'd kill... he'd do whatever it took.

"So, we're watching Fallon then?" Aimee whispered as Brie and Gideon walked up to them.

"Yeah. Since tonight's the full moon hunt and we already ran last night, they asked if we could." He winced as he looked at her. "I'm so used to saying yes when it comes to family that I didn't ask you. I'm sorry."

She took his hand and shrugged. "Say yes all the time, Walker. I'll do the same if they ask me. They're family." Something he wasn't sure she was used to beyond her friends, but that was something they would get into later. She still hadn't contacted her family, and he wasn't sure if she would. She'd said they weren't close, and the evidence of that was mounting day by day.

Before he could talk about that, however, his brother and family were standing in front of him.

"Thank you so much for watching Fallon," Brie said with a smile. "She wants to hunt but is still too young to be out with the big wolves." She kissed Fallon's nose, and the little girl snuggled into her mom's hold.

"It's really no problem," Aimee said, waving at Fallon, who in turn held out her arms. Aimee held the little girl close and smiled, bringing images to mind of her doing that with *their* child.

They were already moving fast, but it was the male in him just then that couldn't wait for that vision to become real in truth.

Gideon must have known the direction of his thoughts because his big brother just gave him a knowing grin.

"Have fun on your hunt," Walker said dryly.

"We're going outside the den wards through our territory again, but we'll be close in case you need us."

Walker nodded. "I was planning on taking the ladies for a walk under the moon if that's okay."

"You should be safe in the clearing near us. It's guarded, and a lot of the pups will be out there with their sitters since it's not good to keep everyone trapped within the magic for days on end."

That was the problem with wards sometimes. It kept people out, but it also kept their own people in, and that was stifling for anyone, especially a pup. The night of the hunt was the best time to take them out in groups since everyone was just slightly stronger on full moon nights. And, thankfully, they wouldn't be in the clearing they'd been attacked in before. He'd rather not make Aimee relive that anytime soon.

She was healthy, the curse was gone, and she was his. There was nothing to worry about.

The other couple headed to where the hunt would be, and Walker took his girls to the clearing—a different one from the night before as that one was just for the two of them for now. As he watched Fallon run around with Aimee, he couldn't help but think how much his life had changed in the past few months. He'd been the one Brentwood in search of a mate and securing the bonds themselves, and when that hadn't happened, fate had brought Aimee to him in the most unexpected way.

Their lives were far from settled, and there were still so many unanswered questions when it came to her curse and this new form of hers, but for the time being, he was...happy.

He met Aimee's eyes as Fallon bounced around in her little wolf form, yipping and barking like an adorable wolf pup, then froze as an eerily familiar magic hit the air.

"Aimee, down!" he yelled and slammed to the ground himself, arm-crawling toward his mate and niece.

His mate had thrown herself over Fallon as fire burned over them from four directions—the same curse that had come for Parker. Only this time, the fire didn't reach down. It was as if this were a warning, not a full-scale attack.

He could hear others around them shouting and screaming, their feet hitting hard on the ground as they ran, but Walker knew it would be too late.

This wasn't the same curse as before, he'd been wrong. He met Aimee's gaze, made his way to her, and gripped her hand.

"Hold on," he yelled. They watched the fire, not hot like before but cool, almost as if it were in a vacuum—or rather, the vacuum itself. There was a small opening where someone could escape—someone far smaller than he or Aimee.

"Fallon, honey, I need you to run through that hole and don't look back until you see someone you know. Can you do that?"

His niece looked at him with eyes far wiser than she should have, but then again, she was the future Alpha and carried within her a power he could never hope to comprehend.

"Go. Find your parents." Fallon reached out, cupped his face with one tiny hand, then crawled away before running full-tilt on her tiny toddler legs. Out of the corner of his eye, he saw another soldier pick her up almost immediately outside of the fire zone, but Walker couldn't see anything else.

It was as if the spell had made a cross and marked the spot where Aimee and Walker lay. He held his mate, and the fire lowered and lowered until, eventually, it brushed against them, not hot, but so cold that it felt as if he were burning from frostbite instead of flame.

He couldn't move, couldn't think, and as the screaming started, he held his mate and thought of nothing else.

He'd been happy. Hopeful.

But in the end, he'd been wrong.

CHAPTER 17

AIMEE WOKE UP WITH A START, her body feeling
as though she were bruised all over. It took a second for
her to remember what had happened.

Walker.

She needed to find Walker. There had been flames
that weren't flames, and Fallon had made it to safety.
Then, everything had been so cold, and she'd held onto
Walker as the world darkened. She couldn't remember
anything beyond that. Somehow, she wasn't where she'd
been when the fire slid over the sky. She was instead in a
new location, one that didn't smell familiar. Of course, she
was so new to these senses, she could be wrong.

She turned her head, only to be forced to hold back
bile as her stomach revolted from the quick movement.
After sucking in a breath, letting the cold air clear her

head, she opened her eyes, unaware that she'd had them closed the whole time, and froze.

Walker sat across from her but far enough away that she couldn't reach him. Someone had torn his shirt off, and long lines of burns and cuts covered his chest, blood seeping slowly from the wounds. From the looks of it, he was unconscious, his arms raised above his head and secured by manacles and chains that looked as though they'd come from some movie about medieval torture chambers.

Fearing the worst, she kept her gaze on him until she could clearly see his chest rise and fall with his breaths. She could also feel him through the mating bond, but she was still so new to that, she was afraid to truly trust it.

That's when she noticed the chains on his ankles. Whoever had taken them—most likely the fire witch and Blade—they hadn't wanted Walker to escape. She looked down at her own legs and noticed that they were unchained, but her arms were secured above her head as his were. Whoever had made the metal did a good job, because even with her newfound strength, she couldn't get free.

"I wouldn't try that if I were you," an unfamiliar voice said from beside her. Aimee turned to see a woman with long, white hair and black robes moving toward her. She was truly beautiful, but there was an edge to her that frightened Aimee. Not to mention that the magic crackling in the air was familiar...but it wasn't that of the fire witch. No, this was another magic user, and Aimee had a feeling the reason she could almost recognize the magic was because it had been rooted inside her body for as long as she could remember.

This was the witch who had cursed her.

And she wasn't happy.

"Scarlett and Blade have plans for the wolf, but as for you, they've given you to me as a present. I don't normally take gifts from other witches, but since you've been on my radar for some time now, I might just take them up on it."

"Having time for a monologue, are you, Chloe?" A woman with long, red hair and a skintight, red dress prowled through the door behind the witch, a man who looked to have some power but didn't taste of Alpha by her side. Aimee didn't know what was going on, but she had a bad feeling she was about to find out.

Chloe shrugged. "It's about time she realizes what she is to me and why she shouldn't go around breaking curses she knows nothing about. She's lucky she survived the separation in the first place, but now that she's here... well, I'll make sure she doesn't do it again." She raised her chin at the other witch. "And, Scarlett, darling, you're the queen of monologues, taking this bad witch thing as far as making sure your dresses match your mood... I mean, really, a red dress for a red witch? How cliché."

"Now, ladies..."

Both Chloe and Scarlett glared at the man with them, and he shut up quickly. Definitely not Blade, then. She knew of no Alpha who would back down that quickly unless their mate looked at him that way.

"Keep your mate quiet, Scarlett. He's annoying me."

Scarlett just rolled her eyes and patted her mate on the ass like he was just a piece of meat to her. There was no love in their interactions, no way for them to show off their bond like Aimee had seen others do; like she did herself when it came to Walker.

"You're the one who cursed me," Aimee said, gathering her courage. She wasn't about to go down without a fight. She had spent too much of her life already on the defense rather than fighting for herself.

"Of course, I am. I'm Chloe, an air witch far older than you are, darling."

"What did I ever do to you? Why did you curse me?"

"It wasn't you, it was the blood that runs in your veins. Didn't you ever wonder about your family and how nothing ever worked right for them? I found your grandfather when he was young and knew he was goddess-blessed. She does that to some humans, you know, blesses them because, apparently, they have some important part to play in fate. It's rare, and even rarer for a witch to find and be able to use. Because of your blessings, I was able to use the curse to steal your luck, your fate, and your energy so I could live longer. And when you started to fade long before your time, well, let's just say I wasn't happy. I've been on the hunt for another family I could drain because you were my prize and yet you were far too *weak* to last long."

Aimee couldn't believe her ears. This woman was so selfish that she'd cursed an entire family for her own greed. And Chloe wasn't done, apparently.

"When you broke the curse—something that shouldn't have happened by the way—you stole my future. It's not fair that the moon goddess only lets mates of shifters and shifters themselves become immortal. She should have gifted the witches, as well. And because of that, I took what was *mine*. She should have blessed all of us, not just a few humans who didn't know what they had."

"I guess you're lucky you had me," Scarlett's mate said, his voice soft. He looked soft, as well, and Aimee wasn't sure what it was about him, but she had a feeling the fire witch had broken him long ago. Fate could be cruel it seemed—on both sides of the coin.

"I guess so," Scarlett said with a shrug as if she didn't care. "You get to keep your little lion, but remember that you work for us now. Got it? I could have killed her right away and said 'screw you' to your little curse and long life, but I'm a giver."

Chloe snorted. "Sure, honey. And I'm the witch Easter bunny. Watch me hop." She gestured toward Walker, who was just now stirring. Whatever they had done to him when Aimee was unconscious must have been bad, and she had to swallow back the bile that rose in her throat. "What are you going to do with that one? Looks like you already played a little."

Flames danced around Scarlett's fingers as she flicked them as if she were playing with a coin, the way Aimee's father had long ago when he was happier and liked doing parlor tricks. It hurt to think that his happiness had been taken away because of the witch in front of her.

"Blade wants him dead, and for an example to be made. I don't mind, as it keeps my skills sharp." She slid her red-hot fingers over the edge of a blade on the counter near them as if she were telling a little joke as she spoke.

They were laughing as if his life meant nothing to them. As if he were just a toy for them to play with instead of the mate she loved and the one she had vowed to protect as she'd marked him as hers.

Power like nothing she'd ever felt before slid through her, and she stood, her legs sure and no longer shaky. When the trio turned to her, she didn't give them time to wonder what she was going to do. Instead, she tugged at the chains, letting her cat come to the surface and show in her eyes.

Before the others could react, the chains snapped from the wall. Walker stirred then, and she knew he was waking, could feel it along the bond, but she wasn't done yet.

They should have tied her feet as they had his.

They'd made a mistake.

And they would pay for it.

The witches mumbled something under their breaths, but Aimee was faster. She slammed one end of the chain into Scarlett's face, and she screamed, knocked back into her mate. Aimee took the other chain and wrapped it around the air witch's neck twice, then pulled. Without air, the witch could do nothing, and without breath, the witch would die at Aimee's hands.

So be it.

Aimee tugged and pulled, her cat at the forefront as the air witch weakened under her strength. The chain tightened again, and she looked up to see Walker pulling on the other end, keeping Chloe in place. He could barely do it with what little slack they'd given him, but with his help, the air witch fell to the floor, purple mottling her neck, and her gaze empty.

Scarlett went to scream something at them, and Aimee jumped from the counter where she'd landed in her haste and threw herself over Walker. Scarlett didn't have time to finish her curse, however, because the door slammed open, and Gideon and Brie stood in the opening where it had fallen off its hinges.

The cavalry had arrived.

And Momma Wolf was *pissed.*

CHAPTER 18

WALKER HAD NEVER BEEN HAPPIER to see his Alpha and sister-in-law in his life. Still chained and hurting from whatever the fuck Scarlett had done to him, he tried to hold onto his mate, but she was having none of it.

The room filled with Talons as Kameron, Parker, Avery, Brandon, and Max stormed into the small dungeon after Gideon and Brie. Somehow, the magic of the fire had spat him and Aimee there. Aimee was trying to pull the chains off him but couldn't reach. Max was there to help one-handed and was so full of rage, the manacles broke in his hand.

As Aimee tried to help Walker stand, other wolves not of his Pack who smelled like Aspens filled the room, and the fight began.

If it weren't for Fallon almost being hurt like she had been, Walker knew Brie wouldn't have come to fight alongside Gideon. It wasn't that she wasn't allowed and didn't know how to fight, it was that her wolf fought in different ways. It was easier for every dominant around if she stayed behind to be protected while she protected them when they got home—even from themselves.

But she was beyond enraged, and he could see the wolf in her gaze—something he didn't see often when it came to her. She and Gideon fought like they'd been alongside one another for centuries, rather than the few short years they'd been together. Kameron was going after the fire witch, but as he went to claw her neck, the witch's mate—who Walker now knew was also some kind of cat shifter—stood in front of her, taking the blow. By some stroke of luck, Kameron's claws slid through his artery and, without a Healer, Walker knew the man wouldn't make it. Then, when Kameron slid his claw down to the cat's heart, it was over.

The witch screamed, and the other fights in the room froze for a bare moment as Walker leaned heavily into Max as Aimee held him up on his left.

Fire slammed into the walls surrounding Scarlett, burning her own wolves as the Talons ducked. As a witch, her life was tied to her mate's, and though she wouldn't die right away, she might only have minutes or hours to live depending on the mating bond they'd shared.

Kameron had not only killed the cat but also the witch.

However, from the looks of it, she wasn't going down without a fight.

"We need to get out of here," Aimee called out over the roar of flames. "The whole place is going up in flames."

"Come on," Max said, half dragging him. Walker was out of energy, and it was only because of his fight for Aimee that he'd been able to help her take out Chloe.

The Talons left the others where they fell and scrambled back to their trucks where they'd somehow used the bonds to find him and Aimee. They weren't on Aspen land, and he hadn't been able to scent Blade or even Audrey, so he had no idea where they were.

But he was damned thankful that they'd come.

That his mate had been stronger than he'd thought possible.

Fire licked up the walls and poured through the windows as they drove off, then the building where he'd been chained too far away from his mate to touch her and make sure she was alive exploded into a thousand shards.

Taking the shifters inside with it.

And, perhaps, just maybe, the witch as well.

The others spoke, asking him questions and talking about battle plans, but he could only hold onto Aimee, gritting through the pain. Leah would be able to help later, but for now, he would just breathe. Just be.

The Aspens had declared war, even if they didn't know it.

Nothing would be the same.

Ever.

BLOOD BOUND

BLADE CARRIED Scarlett's beaten and battered body to one of his strongholds and cursed. He needed her for his plans, and he'd be damned if he lost her because she'd lost her mate. She wasn't his mate, and he couldn't keep her alive that way, but there were other ways. The air witch had been alive for over a century after all, hadn't she?

"Wake up," he growled. She looked up at him from under sooty lashes and glared. "How do we use your magic to keep you alive like Chloe did?"

His witch let out a pained breath and sat up, holding out her wrist. "It won't be the same magic, but I can blood bond to you. Not a mating bond," she added quickly. "And I won't take your life force. You're connected to the Pack, so it'll slowly draw power through the Pack bonds without killing anyone." She paused. "Maybe. But it's going to hurt."

"I'll own you," he spat, holding out his wrist and giving her a knife. She'd said blood, and that meant there needed to be cutting, something she liked to do with molten-hot knives if he remembered right.

She met his gaze. "You already do, don't you?"

She'd been right. It had hurt. She'd screamed, and he'd held in his own, not wanting to show weakness, but when she was through and the magic had worked its way over him, he knew she was bound to him in a way she hadn't been before. The Pack wouldn't be happy about this, but he'd blame the Talons.

He'd blame the air witch and that little lion the fucking Brentwoods now had in their arsenal. He'd blame Audrey, and when he was done teaching her a lesson, she'd blame herself.

He was done letting others do the dirty work for him. All they'd done was make mistake after mistake. It was time for the Talons to know whom they were messing with. And when they figured it out, it would be too late.

Finally.

EPILOGUE

WALKER SLID INTO AIMEE, their hands clasped as they moved as one. Their bodies were healed and whole, and now joined as they made love under the moonlight as it shone through the open window in their bedroom. She arched into him, and he took her mouth, increasing his speed as he thrust in and out of her.

She clung to him, her claws digging into his back, pushing his wolf even more.

After they'd come, they lay sweaty, spent, and tangled with one another, their chests heaving as they panted.

"Round four?" she mumbled, her eyes closed.

Walker let out a strained laugh. "That was already round five. I think my dick is sore."

"Aw, poor baby." She reached between them and patted his length. "Does he need a kiss to make it better?"

He covered her hand with his and brought it up to his lips for a kiss. "Away, woman. You'll break me."

"We wouldn't want that." She kissed him again, this time lazily.

"We're going to be late for the Pack meeting," he said after they were both calm, yet hadn't moved from their positions in the bed.

"True, but this is very comfortable."

He bit her neck gently, and she purred. He could *really* get used to this whole purring thing. When she did it when he was inside of her? Well, let's just say he came like he was a teenager getting used to sex again rather than the man he was.

When she pinched his butt, he laughed and then rolled over, pulling her on top of him. "I think I like this position," he said warmly.

She rolled her eyes, kissed him, then moved to get off the bed. "I thought your dick hurt."

"True, but we could push through."

"So romantic." Then she sashayed over to the bathroom, careful to lock the door behind her. Considering that they'd started this whole bout of sex in the shower earlier that day, he couldn't blame her. They really needed to make it to the Pack meeting since the elders wanted to talk to the two of them beforehand. Shit, they needed to get a move on.

Walker ran to the guest room and quickly showered there before pulling on some jeans and a flannel, button-down that Aimee loved. When he met her in the living room, he couldn't help but stare at her, his attention solely on her as always. She'd put on jeans and a flowy shirt that emphasized her breasts and her healthy curves.

He loved the way she'd filled out. Hell, he'd loved the way she looked before, too. But now, she was healthy and no longer cursed. The air witch was dead and could no longer hurt her or her family—the same family she was starting to contact more. He was grateful for that. Maybe without the magic of the air witch on their shoulders, the others could move on and have a decent life.

He was going to do his damnedest to make sure Aimee had hers.

"Ready?" she asked, practically bouncing. Walker had energy, but Aimee had it in spades. She was already training with Kameron to see if she was truly a soldier, and it had only been about a week since everything happened. She was seriously thriving, and his triplet was ecstatic to have a secret weapon in his arsenal. As long as Aimee was safe and could take care of herself, Walker was fine. If she got hurt in training, however, then he might just have to kick Kameron's ass. Out of principle, of course.

He and Aimee made their way to where the Pack

planned to have their meeting to discuss what would happen within the den, and how the Aspen's new threat would affect them all. There had been no news from Audrey, nor had Blade taken credit for what Scarlett and her mate did. They all knew Blade was behind it all, but since the Alpha hadn't been there in person, there was also plausible deniability.

War where they had to be careful of what the humans saw was a whole different animal than how they'd been able to protect their dens in the past. If his Pack wasn't careful and they attacked the Aspens openly, they could end up in worse trouble with the government and the humans around them. It was a guessing game, one where they had to be strategic, but he believed in his Pack and his family and knew they would find a way to protect everyone.

Xavior and a few of the other elders stood by a group of trees near the Pack meeting place. Not all the elders went to the meetings since some were so old, living in the present was hard for them, but Xavior went to them more often than not. They didn't have many elders because of what had happened in the past with Walker's father, but the Pack was getting better. Slowly.

"Ah, you're here." The older wolf said with a wink. He looked the same age as Walker, until you looked him in the eyes and saw the depth of knowledge and age within. "I see you've been busy."

Walker let out a low growl. Elder or not, *no one* would be allowed to embarrass his mate.

"Walker," Aimee whispered.

He squeezed her hand then inclined his head. "You wanted to see us?"

The others introduced themselves to Aimee, but it was Xavior who spoke. "When Gideon told us about Aimee's family being goddess-blessed, it helped us remember something. When you two mated, her power was introduced to the Pack through your mating bonds. Because of that, her *blessing* was also introduced."

Walker froze. "The mating bonds. That's how they're healing and how others are starting to see who their mates are or could be again."

"Because of my family?" Aimee asked, sounding as shocked as he was.

"The blood in your veins, yes. By having another goddess-blessed within the Pack, and because she is mated to another goddess-blessed, it seems to be healing the bonds. It will take time, and we don't know what will happen in the future, but it seems that the mating bonds are righting themselves." Xavior frowned. "Or, at least, finding that new normal where they are more easily recognized. I wouldn't be surprised if they are different

altogether, but not as...shattered as they once wore."
There was a howl in the distance, and the elder nodded.
"We're needed at the Pack circle. We can talk more of this
later."

And with that, they left without another word, leaving
Walker and Aimee reeling.

"We...we did that?" Aimee asked, her voice hoarse.
"Others will be able to find their mates now?"

Walker grinned and brought her in for a kiss. "That
sounds about right. I can't believe it. All that research to
see what we could do, and it seemed the moon goddess
and fate already knew how to fix it. She brought me you."

Aimee smiled, her eyes going bright with her cat. "I'm
pretty sure she brought you to me."

He kissed her again, needing her taste even though
they had to leave soon. "I love you, my mate."

"Love you, too, my wolf."

And he kissed her again, ignoring the second warning
howl. He had his mate in his arms, and a future where
they could flourish. He'd been searching for his purpose
for long enough to know that what he needed was in his
arms and in his path. His mate was strong—stronger than
she thought she could be. A fighter who never backed
down. And he was who he was always meant to be. A
Healer, a mate, and a protector.

And if he had fate to thank for that, then, well, he'd

just have to find a way to make that happen—as long as he had Aimee by his side in the end.

UP NEXT:

Find out what happens between Kameron and Dhani in
STRENGTH ENDURING

A NOTE FROM CARRIE ANN

Thank you so much for reading **ETERNAL MOURNING**. I do hope if you liked this story, that you would please leave a review! Reviews help authors *and* readers.

I hope you loved Walker and Aimee's story. They helped me through so much and their story was much sweeter than most Talons but it suited them perfectly!

Next up is Kameron and Dhani and oh my, you guys, just wait until you see what happens between the two of them. I don't know if I'm prepared with what's going to happen, but I better batten down the hatches and get it done!

Of course, if you're doing the math, you know the last book is about our dear Max.

And his story?

Just wait.

If you want to make sure you know what's coming next from me, you can sign up for my newsletter at www.CarrieAnnRyan.com; follow me on twitter at @CarrieAnnRyan, or like my Facebook page. I also have a Facebook Fan Club where we have trivia, chats, and other goodies. You guys are the reason I get to do what I do and I thank you.

Make sure you're signed up for my MAILING LIST so you can know when the next releases are available as well as find giveaways and FREE READS.

Happy Reading!

The Talon Pack:

Book 1: Tattered Loyalties

Book 2: An Alpha's Choice

Book 3: Mated in Mist

Book 4: Wolf Betrayed

Book 5: Fractured Silence

Book 6: Destiny Disgraced

Book 7: Eternal Mourning

Book 8: Strength Enduring

Book 9: Forever Broken

ABOUT THE AUTHOR

Carrie Ann Ryan is the New York Times and USA Today bestselling author of contemporary, paranormal, and young adult romance. Her works include the Montgomery Ink, Redwood Pack, Fractured Connections, and Elements of Five series, which have sold over 3.0 million books worldwide. She started writing while in graduate school for her advanced degree in chemistry and hasn't stopped since. Carrie Ann has written over seventy-five novels and novellas with more in the works. When she's not losing herself in her emotional and action-packed worlds, she's reading as much as she can while wrangling her clowder of cats who have more followers than she does.

www.CarrieAnnRyan.com

ALSO FROM THIS AUTHOR

The Montgomery Ink: Boulder Series:

The Montgomery Ink: Fort Collins Series:

The Less Than Series:

Book 0.5: Ink Inspired
Book 0.6: Ink Reunited
Book 1: Delicate Ink
Book 1.5: Forever Ink
Book 2: Tempting Boundaries
Book 3: Harder than Words
Book 4: Written in Ink
Book 4.5: Hidden Ink
Book 5: Ink Enduring
Book 6: Ink Exposed
Book 6.5: Adoring Ink
Book 6.6: Love, Honor, & Ink
Book 7: Inked Expressions
Book 7.3: Dropout
Book 7.5: Executive Ink
Book 8: Inked Memories
Book 8.5: Inked Nights
Book 8.7: Second Chance Ink

The Gallagher Brothers Series:

Book 1: Love Restored
Book 2: Passion Restored
Book 3: Hope Restored

The Whiskey and Lies Series:

Book 1: Whiskey Secrets

Book 2: Whiskey Reveals

Book 3: Whiskey Undone

The Talon Pack:

Book 1: Tattered Loyalties

Book 2: An Alpha's Choice

Book 3: Mated in Mist

Book 4: Wolf Betrayed

Book 5: Fractured Silence

Book 6: Destiny Disgraced

Book 7: Eternal Mourning

Book 8: Strength Enduring

Book 9: Forever Broken

Redwood Pack Series:

Book 1: An Alpha's Path

Book 2: A Taste for a Mate

Book 3: Trinity Bound

Book 3.5: A Night Away

Book 4: Enforcer's Redemption

Book 4.5: Blurred Expectations

Book 4.7: Forgiveness

Book 5: Shattered Emotions

Book 6: Hidden Destiny

Book 6.5: A Beta's Haven

Book 7: Fighting Fate

Book 7.5: Loving the Omega

Book 7.7: The Hunted Heart

Book 8: Wicked Wolf

The Branded Pack Series:
(Written with Alexandra Ivy)

Book 1: Stolen and Forgiven

Book 2: Abandoned and Unseen

Book 3: Buried and Shadowed

Dante's Circle Series:

Book 1: Dust of My Wings

Book 2: Her Warriors' Three Wishes

Book 3: An Unlucky Moon

Book 3.5: His Choice

Book 4: Tangled Innocence

Book 5: Fierce Enchantment

Book 6: An Immortal's Song

Book 7: Prowled Darkness

Book 8: Dante's Circle Reborn

Holiday, Montana Series:

Book 1: Charmed Spirits

Book 2: Santa's Executive

Book 3: Finding Abigail

Book 4: Her Lucky Love

Book 5: Dreams of Ivory

The Happy Ever After Series:
Flame and Ink
Ink Ever After

Single Title:
Finally Found You